STARING DOWN THE DRAGON

by Dorothea N. Buckingham

This story had many guides. My thanks to Dr. B. Alan Shoupe, pediatric oncologist at Tripler Army Medical Center, Honolulu, Hawaii for sharing his medical expertise and for treating his patients with hope, laughter and prayer. To Dr. Jeanne Hoffman, psychologist, who counsels families of children with life-threatening diseases. To nurses Norma Meyer, Kim Kiakona, Sharlene Silva and librarians Nina O'Donnell and Melode Reinke for their reading. To Evelyn and Rick Maldonado who shared their son with the world for six short years. To Patricia Bourgeois, a teen cancer survivor, and an author in her own right, for her input. To Sarah Yasutake for her edit of this book. To her mother, Virginia Wageman, for her strong spirit in fighting the dragon. To Brian Miyamoto for cover photography. To Julie DeMello, who comes from a long line Cabral and DeMello woman, for modeling for this cover.

To readers, Charlie and Nicole Buckingham, Patricia Nelson, Wanda Castellaw, Carly Shoupe, Catherine Reynolds and Mitsu Papayoanou. To Caroline Spencer for funky earrings and lifetime support. To all who have been a part of this project, I offer my thanks and gratitude. And to Jack Buckingham, my husband, my anchor, my support, Shantih.

Requests for permission for use should be directed to:
Sydney Press
258 Aikane Street
Kailua, Hawaii 96734-1603

This book is a work of fiction. Any references to real people or real locations are fiction. Any resemblance to actual events, locales or persons, living or dead is coincidental.

Buckingham, Dorothea N.
Staring Down the Dragon

Summary: Fifteen-year old Rell DeMello returns to high school after having been successfully treated for cancer. Adjustments must be made with family, friends and her own self-identity.

[1. Cancer - Fiction. 2. Life changing events - Fiction. 2. Family relationships - Fiction.]
I. Title
ISBN 0-9724577-3-9
LCCN 2002094635

Cover design: Kennedy & Preiss Graphic Design
Book design: Eric Papayoanou
Editor: Sarah Wageman Yasutake

Printed in Canada

For Charlie and Al

CHAPTER ONE

He walked for fifteen minutes before he thought
he came to it. "Cross it," she said and he
thought there would be a bridge of some sort.
There was none.

—Toni Morrison, *Song of Solomon*

I didn't know what to wear my first day back at school. I
wanted to look fantastic—better than fantastic—I wanted to
look like I never had cancer. That was it, I "had" cancer like I
"had" a broken leg in seventh grade. And now that treatment
was over, I could get back to being just me, Rell DeMello.

Enter memories: me in fifth grade, dancing hula in the
Lei Day Pageant; me in seventh grade, captain of the soccer
team, sitting on the sidelines with my cast. And last
September—me at the beginning of sophomore year not
knowing I was sick.

Before September I never used the word cancer. It was
something old people got, and most of them died. But by
April I could have done a science project on it, complete
with myself as show and tell.

When I was in treatment at Stanhope Hospital in San
Francisco, I used to dream about coming home to Hawai'i. I
dreamed about sitting at the beach, driving around with Emi
and playing with my dog. I saw myself walking back into

school on my first day back—kids would pile me with leis so high you couldn't see my face. There'd be a "Welcome Home, Rell" banner in big red letters painted on a white sheet hanging from the front door. I even practiced the speech I would give at my Welcome Back assembly. But when the day came for me to go back, I didn't want any banners or assembly. All I wanted to do was to sneak back to my old desk and pretend that nothing had ever happened.

Going back to school after being treated for cancer wasn't like the first day after summer vacation. I didn't think any teachers would ask me to write an essay on what I did on my chemotherapy vacation.

I was afraid I'd be assigned a special seat, like Ella Cunha who wears two hearing aids and sits in the front row for every class. I knew I looked different. I wore a wig, I'd lost twenty pounds and I had a Frankenstein scar on my neck. I was afraid kids would stare, and I was afraid of them asking me questions.

On the Sunday night before I went back to school I spent an hour smiling in front of the mirror. I tilted my head and told jokes to myself about the guys in the hospital. I made up stories about riding the cable cars in San Francisco and eating chocolate at Ghirardelli Square; then I told stories about having cancer and made it sound like a bad case of the flu.

When the day came, my mother drove me to school in her two-door, beige Saturn. She drove right up to the front of the building. Kids parted like the Red Sea. I dove down to the floor to tie my shoes.

Mom pulled up to the steps. The only thing missing was

a Day-Glo handicapped sign painted on the door, or maybe a bullhorn announcing I was back.

"It's going to be okay," Mom said.

"I know." I zipped up my backpack.

"It really will." She rubbed my back, then she leaned over and kissed me. "I love you, Rell." She said it like it had some kind of magical power.

"I love you, too, Mom."

I slung my backpack over my shoulder and inched out of the car. I took a deep breath, stood tall and headed up the steps. I stared at the front door—the heavy, gray, metal door.

"Good luck, Sweetheart," Mom yelled from the car.

I looked back. She waved and threw me a kiss like she was the grand marshal of the Mother Love Parade.

"Smile, Rell," I told myself. "Just smile."

Kailua High School's two-story building looked like a towering castle. I climbed the steps, working my way through swarms of kids getting in a last blast of a CD or a last grinding kiss. I hugged my backpack to my chest to keep anyone from bumping into me.

It was like they were in a fast-forward video and I was in slow motion. I got to the door, put my hand on the handle, turned and walked down the steps and headed straight to McDonald's, where I spent the rest of the day.

That afternoon when Mom picked me up, she leaned over and kissed me again. "How did it go today, Sweetheart?" She stroked the back of my neck. She was always careful not to touch my wig.

"It was great, Mom." I tossed my backpack in the back

seat.

"You look a little tired, Rell." She had one of her oh-my-poor-baby looks on her face.

At forty-three years old, my mother looked more like a college student than a college professor. She was tall and thin with dark wavy hair and olive skin that never had a zit. I inherited her hair and skin but my build was all my father's. "Athletic" is what the magazines called it. Of course, that was before my chemotherapy. After treatment I was supermodel thin.

"How about a little celebration for your first day back?" Mom said. "We can stop at McDonald's."

"No, thanks." The only thing I could order at McD's was super-sized trouble.

"We could go to Jamba Juice or Maui Taco."

"I'm really not hungry, Mom."

"You need something in your stomach," she said.

If my mother couldn't kiss cancer away she was going to feed it to death.

"Not even a shake?"

"No, Mom. Honest."

"You do look a little tired."

"I'm not tired and I'm not hungry." What I was, was scared that she wouldn't drive away before one of my friends came out and asked me what I was doing at school.

Mom took off her sunglasses and fumbled through her purse for I have no idea what. She opened it wide and angled it toward herself.

Will you please hurry up! I was thinking it so loud I was

sure she could hear me. Hurry, before Emi sees me.

"Did you get to see most of your friends?"

"Uh-huh."

What is she looking for?

She shook her purse and dug deep inside. "Want some gum?" She lifted it in the air.

I shook my head.

"Rell, do you think you can catch up on your school work?"

I wanted to scream, "Drive!" But I said, "I think so. The hospital tutor was better than I thought." My lies were getting bigger.

"And the rest of your day?"

"As the doctors say, it was 'uneventful.'" She shot me one of those that's-not- funny-young-lady looks.

Just then Paul Cruz banged the front of the car with his hand and waved. I waved back. Nate Lee was right behind him.

"Kids seem to be happy to see you." She put the car in gear.

"Paul's in a few of my classes."

She edged into traffic. "And the other guy?"

"He's a junior."

She pulled away. I was safe.

"Did you see Emi?"

"We had lunch together."

"And?" She turned to me.

"She met a new guy this weekend. Some basketball player from St. Luke's." I named Emi's imaginary boyfriend Grant. I made him six foot two inches tall, a hundred eighty pounds, fair skinned with a mole on his left cheek. "She'll probably get him to ask her to their Spring Carnival, then she'll dump him."

"Do you have much homework?"

"Not too much," I answered.

"Did Mr. Owens talk to you?" she asked.

Mr. Owens was the school counselor.

"He told me he would give you a health room pass to use if you got tired."

"When did he say that?"

"Last week."

They talked last week. My heart moved from my chest to my throat and was quickly working its way to my mouth.

"He was supposed to give you some paperwork I have to mail to Stanhope."

I'm dead meat.

"Rell." She looked over to me as she was driving. "Did you thank everyone for their cards?"

"Yes."

With each question I answered I was rewarded with another: Did you remember to pick up the form for your yearbook picture? What did you eat for lunch? Did you meet the exchange student from Brazil? And, finally, Did anyone say anything that upset you?

Only you, Mom.

I was sick of questions. I craved a day with no questions—no questions, no charts, no poking, no prodding and no curiosity about my condition. One whole day when no one cared if I was tired, hungry, constipated or dead.

"How was school for you, Mom?" It was a lateral

pass. An offensive move. "The best defense is a good offense." That's what Dad said when he talked about negotiating a deal. "You've got to catch the other guy off guard."

"Terrific." She smiled. "Dr. Kosaki assigned me all online classes next semester. This way when we go back to Stanhope for your follow-up tests, or if anything happens, I can teach from there, like I did last semester."

I knew we would be going back to Stanhope for follow-up tests, but I also knew what "if anything happens" meant. It meant if my cancer came back.

I stared out the window at the new coffee shop that opened next to Safeway.

"What about math class?" Mom said. "You've always had trouble with math."

"Math's okay," I said. I got a whiff of the coffee from the shop. Hula Brew. Cute name.

"Dad has an intern from the university working for him. He's an engineering student. I'm sure he could help you with math."

"I'll think about it." *Great—a geek engineer wannabe who would spy for my father.*

"You're not very strong in math, Rell." Mom pulled in to the driveway.

I'm even weaker in showing up at school.

"Just once, I'd like the paper in the driveway and not under the hedge." Mom shut down the car and gathered up her things.

"I'll get it." The mock orange hedge was in full bloom. As I reached under it I took in a breath of its almost-too-sweet smell.

When I was at Stanhope, LB was my best friend. Sometimes after chemotherapy treatment when she thought her skin smelled like her drugs I described the smell of mock orange, ginger or plumeria. And when she said her food tasted like copper, I told her about the taste of huli-huli chicken, fresh from the grill.

"Rell." Mom was leaning against the gate with her briefcase wedged against it. Her purse was dangling from her elbow and she had her books clutched to her chest. "Could you bring in the mail, Sweetheart?"

I grabbed my backpack and headed to the mailbox.

"Ajax, get down!" Mom yelled at the dog. "Get down!" The dog jumped up on her, then circled around her legs. "This nonsense has got to stop! It has got to stop." She repeated herself, slower and louder, as if the dog knew that when she talked like that it meant that he was in big trouble.

He scooted around her.

"Ajax!" I squatted down and put my arms out. "Good boy." I let him lick my face. "Good boy."

I loved Ajax—he never asked me any questions.

"Rell, do not let the dog…" The phone rang inside the house. "Lick your face."

Mom hurried to answer it. Some change spilled out of her purse. "Can you get that, too?"

I was sure it was Mr. Owens on the phone.

I chased a dime and two quarters to the curb. The dime rolled into the sewer. I wished I could follow it down.

I'm dead, I thought. Dead Woman Walking. I picked up

her change, got the mail and shuffled into the kitchen. I was ready for a Mom-explosion.

"Rell, that was Emi on the phone. She'll be right over."

It was Emi. I'm safe.

While Mom got her books and papers organized, I sorted the mail into piles. *Construction Engineering Monthly* for Dad, a *Seventeen* for me, an English journal for Mom and a bill from Stanhope Hospital.

"I'm going to bake some cookies," Mom said. "What are you in the mood for? Oatmeal or chocolate chips?"

"Oatmeal," I answered.

I grabbed my *Seventeen* and headed down the hall to my room. I took off my wig, set it on my lampshade and plopped on the bed. I accidentally caught a glimpse of myself in the mirror—a blue-skinned girl with a high-gloss scalp.

When I was five years old I pulled out all the hair on my Lizzie doll, leaving her with a scalp of empty holes and a few strands of black rayon. I could have passed for Lizzie's older sister.

I leafed through *Seventeen*, searching for bald-headed models with no eyebrows and no eyelashes. There were none.

I craved hair.

Enter fantasy: Running on the beach with my hair billowing in the breeze.

Enter reality: I fell asleep and didn't wake up until Mom called from the kitchen. "Emi's here!"

I dashed to put on my wig. Emi had never seen me without it.

"And just where were you today, Miss Rell?" Emi made her entrance. She stood at my door with her head cocked and her hands on her hips.

"Shh!" I put my finger to my lips.

"Don't shush me." She lifted her eyebrows so high that they disappeared under her bangs.

I pulled her into my room and shut the door.

"I just lied my head off to your mother about your great first day back at school," she said.

"I went to McDonald's," I said.

She widened her eyes. "All day?"

"I was looking for a date."

"Did you find one?"

"His name is Gus. He's seventy. He's got bad breath and walks with a cane and drives a red Miata."

"Cute," Emi said as she stretched herself across my bed. "Seriously, where were you?" She turned on her stomach, folded my pillow in half and tucked it under her chin.

"Seriously, I was at McDonald's."

"Why didn't you come to school?"

"I don't know," I said. "I couldn't face going back in." I shrugged. "When I got out of the car and saw all those kids staring at me." I shrugged again. I could feel the tears creeping out of my eyes.

Emi reached for the box of tissues on my desk and handed them to me. "You okay?"

"What do you think?" I twisted my mouth into half a smile.

"Dumb question," she said.

Emi was my best friend. We met in third grade. We

played on the same soccer team, we quit Girl Scouts on the same day (our first day) and every Fourth of July I went camping with her family.

"What if I picked you up for school tomorrow?" she said. "Then we can walk in to school together."

"That's okay." I shook my head.

"I could pick up Sarah on the way."

"I don't think so."

"The two of us could throw rose petals at your feet as you walk in."

"Not in the plan," I said.

"What about Jonathan Nekoa?" Emi perked up. "Jonathan can walk in front of you blowing a conch shell."

"Enough."

"Imagine." She closed her eyes. "Jonathan in a skinny little malo with the end flapping down."

"And you just waiting for a strong breeze?"

She wiggled her eyebrows.

"You're crazy." I threw a pillow at her.

"You need something to get you going," she said. "What about shopping? You need shopping to get you going."

"I don't like shopping. You like shopping. I hate the mall, remember?"

"Shopping will make you happy."

"No it won't." I could have been talking to the wall.

She flashed a broad smile.

Emi was half-Japanese, half-Hawaiian, tall and lean, with teardrop onyx eyes that disappeared when she smiled. Of the two of us, she was the pretty one. I was the short one with the dark round eyes and a 34B chest. At least I used to have a chest, before treatment.

Emi dug in her purse. "Island Girls is having a closeout sale. Look." She pulled out an ad for boa feather earrings.

I looked at the ad. "They should be giving them away."

"All the movie stars are wearing them, Rell."

Emi knew everything the movie stars were wearing. She knew what they ate for breakfast, who they were dating and who they were cheating on. She bought every celebrity and fashion magazine that Long's Drugs sold. She could fill a toolbox with her earrings, and her bathroom vanity looked like a closeout counter for Cover Girl makeup.

"Yeah, you're right." She crumpled up the ad and tossed it in my wastebasket. "But, I do need to get some lipstick," she said.

Emi wouldn't leave the house without her lips glossed, her cheeks blushed and at least three bracelets on. I hardly ever wore makeup, spent my life in T-shirts and shorts and the closest thing I came to wearing jewelry was carrying around a Diet Coke.

"Will you at least go with me?" Emi asked.

"I don't feel like it."

Emi dug in her purse again, this time pulling out her car keys, jingling them in the air. "We could go to my house after," she said. "No one is home."

"No one?"

"No one."

I gave her a thumbs up.

No adults. No questions. No one worrying about what I was doing.

"Mom," I yelled, "can I go over to Emi's house?"

"And to the mall," Emi added.

"No mall," I said to Emi.

"Yes. Mall," she whispered.

"I can't hear you," Mom yelled back from the kitchen.

In seconds Mom was at the door—kitchen towel in her hand, flour dusted on her apron. "The cookies will be ready in about ten minutes," she said.

"Mom, can I go to the—"

"Mall," Emi finished my sentence.

Mom looked directly at me. She scraped some cookie dough off her fingers. "Estrella, after being at school all day, do you think you should be with more people?"

That's what she said, but what she meant was: "If you go to the mall, a kid with measles, mumps or the bubonic plague will sneeze and you will almost die, and on the way to the hospital an alien, in the form of an emergency medical worker, will inject you with a glowing green serum and kidnap you to Planet 53."

"I'm going to Island Girls to get some lipstick, Mrs. DeMello. Rell doesn't have to come in," Emi said. "Then we're going straight to my house. I promise."

That was another big difference between Emi and me. Emi had an older brother and a younger sister. I was an only child—the only one who could be blamed for drawing cows on the wall or feeding peanut butter to the dog. No brothers, no sisters, no one to distract Mom and Dad from me or my cancer.

"Okay, but be careful." I could hear the doubt in her voice.

"I will," I said.

Emi and I were off to the mall. I hated the mall. I hated it before I got sick and I hated it more after. To be honest, Mom wasn't the only one who was afraid of all those sneezing snot-nosed kids and their nasty germs. I was afraid, too, and I didn't want to be stared at by every jerk who was freaked out by a girl in a wig with no eyebrows or eyelashes. But I told Emi I would go, knowing I would wait in the car.

"Just a second." I went to the bathroom and straightened out my wig.

"Aren't you ready yet?" Emi called out.

"In a minute." I gave the wig a final tug.

When I opened the door, Emi was playing with my Hat-Hair wig.

"This is really neat," she said. She pulled the bangs off the Velcro strip on the visor.

"Yeah, the wig in the back is separate, too." I flipped it over for her. "So you can get long or medium hair if you want, and still keep the bangs the same."

"Do they sell pony tails?" Emi asked.

"I guess," I said. "But then, the sides of your scalp would show and you'd still look bald."

"Neat." Emi balanced the Hat-Hair wig over my lamp and fluffed out the hair with her fingers. "You should draw in a face on the lamp shade."

"You're warped."

"Okay, we're off," she said.

I grabbed my *Seventeen*. "Wait." I flipped it to the makeover article. "Do you think you could pick up some stuff at Island Girls to make me look like this?"

"No worries." She winked.

I knew I should worry.

I got in Emi's car, pulled down the visor and straightened my wig again. I counted my eyelashes. I had five—wispy, wimpy and pale, but they were all mine and soon there would be more.

Emi started the car. "You ready, Miss Rell?"

"I am, Miss Em."

She looked back as she pulled out of the driveway. "You missed big news at school today," she said.

"The gossip gods must be punishing me," I said.

"During first period chemistry Wanda announced that Stacey Larson is pregnant."

"Wow! Is it Darren's?"

"You would think," Emi said. "But, macho-man went around all morning saying, "It's not mine. N-o-t mine.""

"What a jerk."

"No. It was the truth." Emi snickered. "At lunch time big-deal-I-know-all-about-sex Stacey admitted she and Darren never had sex."

"All those camping trips on the North Shore?"

"Separate sleeping bags, and Stacey's sister always went with them."

"In the same tent?" I asked.

"Same tent."

"I don't believe it."

"It gets better." Emi turned to me. "She never had sex with anybody! She told Carole then Carole told Kim and Kim told Wanda. Then it was the CNN headline."

"And all this time I thought I was the world's oldest virgin." I stared out the window.

"I'm three months older, remember?" The light turned red at the intersection by the fire station. Emi pointed to a few bare-chested firefighters washing down their truck.

"I betcha their 'hot,'" I said.

Emi groaned. "If you walked into school with one of those guys on your arm everyone would notice."

I don't want to be noticed. I want to be invisible.

"I wish I could transfer to another school."

"It'll be great going back, Rell. Lots of kids ask about you."

"That's what I'm afraid of." I looked over at my reflection in the car window. "I look like a baby bird in a cheap-ass wig."

"It's an expensive-ass wig. Your father told me so." Emi lowered her voice to mimic my dad's. "Nothing but the best for my Estrella. Only the best."

"I even got the best cancer," I said. I could feel a surge of tears burning my eyes, but I held them back.

"You don't have the best cancer. You have a good cancer," Emi corrected me.

Hodgkin's disease was a "good cancer." As if it were a cancer that did all its homework and colored inside the lines.

I hunched my shoulders and made my voice warble like one of the ladies at church. "Lucky you, Rell," she told me. "Hodgkin's disease is a good cancer."

"But it is," Emi said.

"Good like I should lie down on the street and let an ice cream truck run over me so I can die with an Eskimo Pie smashed in my face?"

"It's over, Rell. Stop it."

It's never over, is what I wanted to say. But there were

some things that Emi didn't understand about cancer. I knew Hodgkin's was a "good cancer." Doctors actually used the word "cured," and sometimes that made me feel guilty—like when I was at Stanhope and I met kids with amputated legs or not such great odds of living, I felt guilty for having an "easy cancer" like Hodgkin's.

Emi pulled into the mall parking lot near the Island Girls shop.

"Let's go." She dashed on some lip-gloss and pulled her hair into a big clip.

"I'm not going in," I said.

"It won't take long. In and out. I promise." She crossed her heart with her fingers.

"I can't."

"Once around the lipsticks." She clasped her hands in prayer. "Come on."

"No." I shook my head.

Emi took a deep breath. "Is it the cheap-ass wig?"

"Something like that," I said.

"Okay," Emi said, "but, next time, you are coming in."

"Next time. I promise." I had my fingers crossed.

She kept the keys in the ignition and turned on the radio. "I'll be right out," she said. "Two minutes. Time me."

Emi dashed across the parking lot. I watched as her glimmering black hair was swinging in the sunlight. I wished I could have hair like that. I pulled down the visor and checked myself out in the mirror. "Swinging hair, glimmering in the sun." Who talks like that? I asked myself. Bald girls was my answer.

I turned on the radio. "Honolulu City Lights" was playing

on the oldies station. I loved the part about the guy leaving Hawai'i who sees the city lights from the plane and lifts his lei to his nose, smelling the jasmine. I thought about LB and how much she would like the smell of jasmine.

"Honolulu City Lights" was over, and so were the next four songs. My eyes were fixed on the mall entrance. I counted the people coming out. I was at twenty-three. It was getting hot in the sun and I wanted to go in the mall to get her.

But what if someone sees me?

So what? I argued with myself. *No one cares what you look like. And even if they do, it's their problem, not yours.*

"No one can make you feel uncomfortable." That's what the hospital psychologist used to say. "Only you can make yourself feel embarrassed."

Then I remembered in sixth grade when the elastic on my bathing suit bottom broke and Tommy Ching told all the boys in school.

But that was in sixth grade, Rell. You're a sophomore in high school now.

But I knew there were kids who still remembered.

I decided to go in. I took a deep breath and got out of the car. I stood up tall, smoothed my shirt, squared my shoulders and marched through the crosswalk. I was halfway across when I heard someone call my name. "Rell?"

A Dodge pickup truck with tinted windows pulled over to the curb.

"Rell. Is that you?"

It was Nate Lee.

If I got out of the car thirty seconds earlier, no one

would have seen me.

Do the math, Rell.

You live on an island.

Everyone goes to the mall.

Someone was bound to see you.

"Hi, Nate." I waved at him with one hand, holding on to my wig with the other. "I'm late." I pointed toward the mall. "I'm meeting Emi. I'm late." And I ran towards the door.

"You're looking good, Rell," he said.

"Thanks." I stood at the mall entrance and waited for what seemed like forever before the automatic doors slid open. When they closed behind me I felt safe.

I found Emi at the Island Girls checkout register.

"Look. It's all for you." She opened a bag filled with bronzers, brushes, mascara and three lipsticks. "You are going to be drop-dead gorgeous when I'm through with you."

She could have used a better choice of words.

"Check this out." She held up daytime glitter.

Emi was into glamour. I was into not being seen.

"I just saw Nate Lee," I said.

"Wait." She dragged me over to a rack of false eyelashes. "What do you think?" she asked.

"No."

She brought them to the register.

"Emi, I won't wear them."

She handed them to the cashier.

"Emi, no."

"You're going to love them."

"No."

I was still saying "no" at her house while she was dragging a kitchen stool into her room.

She ordered me to sit and face the dresser mirror.

I spun the stool away from the mirror. "Emi, I will not wear false eyelashes."

She popped open the box and put one up to her blinking eye.

"Not in a thousand years," I said.

"They would make such a big difference," Emi said.

"I'd look like the waitress at Flamingo's."

"You mean Iris, with the lace handkerchief pinned under her name tag?"

"That would be the one," I said.

"Iris would be so proud of you, Rell."

She put the lashes up to my eyes.

"What if you glue them too close to my real ones so that when I peel them off I take my good ones with them?"

Emi pulled her lip to one side. "Okay. You've got a point." But before she put them back in the box she tried again. "What about for Halloween?"

I counted on my fingers. Five more months. "Maybe," I said.

Emi propped the *Seventeen* against the mirror. "Let's get started," she said. She lined up the cosmetics on her dresser, then she headed to her bathroom for more.

"I told you that Nate Lee said hi to me at the mall, didn't I?" I said.

Emi was kneeling in front of her bathroom sink, rooting

around, making a pile of bottles and boxes on the tile floor. "What did he say?"

"Hi," I answered.

"That was profound," she said standing up, cradling all of her stuff. "Did he have anything else to say? He's never without an opinion."

"He said, quote, 'You're looking good, Rell.'"

Emi dumped the pots of shadows and jars of blush onto her dresser. "Who does he think he is telling you you're looking good?"

"I don't know," I said. "I thought it was kind of sweet. He is a junior."

"He is so-o California."

"I didn't know he was from California. I thought he transferred from St. Luke's."

"He did." Emi dabbed three stripes of foundation on my jaw line then checked the colors in the mirror.

"His truck is nice, too," I said.

"If you like rust and Bondo." Emi ran her fingers over my forehead, under my wig. "Rell, would you mind taking your wig off?" Her voice exposed a tinge of nervousness.

I slipped my hands under the wig's elastic and lifted it off my head. It was the first time that Emi had seen me bald.

Slowly, I spun the stool to face her, but I didn't look up. "Is it what you thought it would look like?"

"Pretty much," she said. "But I need to swivel you around."

I was facing the mirror. I tried not to look at myself. I looked at the poster of the University of Hawai`i Volleyball Team, her Vegas pennant, the photo of Sarah and Emi tacked to the wall, at the stuffed animals that were faded from the sun, the layer of dust on Emi's desk, the floating specks caught in the sun. I looked at everything, everywhere except at the face in the mirror.

"Emi, can you work without me looking in the mirror?"

"Sure." Emi rotated my stool so my back was to it. She picked up a sponge and held her arms in the air. "Are you ready to be beautiful?"

Do you believe in miracles?

Emi angled my chin to the ceiling. "Look up." She dipped the wedge spoon into the foundation.

"Is Nate Lee really from California?" I asked.

"No, he just goes there a lot. While you were at Stanhope he went to San Francisco twice." She patted a sponge under my eye. "He had some family thing going on. I heard his grandfather was dying."

With my chin pointed to the ceiling, my "oh" sounded like a grunt.

"Yeah. He took off from school a week the last time he went." Emi stroked the makeup over my jaw line and neck. "I'm surprised Wanda didn't start a rumor that you two secretly got married."

I desperately clutched Emi's hands with great drama and said, "Emi, I've been lying to you all this time. I never had cancer. Nate and I met in Las Vegas. We got married in an Elvis chapel."

She yanked my jaw to the left. "Don't talk while I'm trying to work on your face."

"You're jealous," I said.

"Jealous of Nate Lee? I don't think so." She swirled a brush into a pot of blush beads and shook the excess into her cupped hand.

"He talked to me at the beginning of the school year," I said. "I think he's cute."

She turned on the radio and sang as she worked—intensely, sometimes within inches of my face.

"Make a long O with your mouth," Emi said.

I stretched out my mouth as she poked at it with the lip brush. It made my nose tingle.

"Now, pout," she said. "No. Not like that. Soft, like before a kiss." She angled my chin. "Pout again."

I tried to talk but each time she told me not to move, so I just sat there and listened to the radio, and Emi's tone-deaf singing. She worked for almost half an hour before she declared me "done."

She stepped back, holding the Seventeen up to my face. She looked at me, then back at the magazine, then looked at me again.

"Voila!" She twirled me to the mirror.

"Oh my God! I look like a porn queen!"

A bald porn queen.

The front door slammed open.

"Emi, could you pull your car in?" It was Emi's brother, Kalani.

"Be right there," she yelled. "Rell, I know it's a little more makeup than you're used to."

"E-mi!" Kalani yelled.

"I said I'll be right there," she yelled back. Emi shoved the magazine in my lap. "Give it a second," she said. "I did a great job, don't you think?"

All I needed were leather boots and a whip.

I looked at the photo in the magazine. On page 173 there was the "Makeup for the Natural Sophisticate." On page 174 was "Vamp for a Night."

By time Emi got back I had wiped most of the glitter off my face.

"Too much?" she asked.

I showed her my fingers caked with iridescent mauve. "Not for MTV."

"Okay," she said. "I'll get serious this time. I just wanted to have some fun."

I shoved the magazine at her. "Page 174—I want the boring makeup."

"It's a perfect match," she said.

The second time around, I faced the mirror while Emi worked. I watched as she lightened the circles under my eyes and drew in real-looking eyebrows. I took notes as she explained how to swirl the brush and blend the concealer under my eye. With each step, a more normal-looking girl began to emerge. And when Emi was finished, a normal-looking girl appeared.

"You're a genius." I hugged her.

Emi buffed her fingernails against her chest then blew on them. "I know."

"It'll be a lot easier going to school," I said.

"You want me to come over tomorrow morning before school?"

"No." I held up my notes. "I think I can do it." I hugged her again. "Em, I can't wait to show my mom," I said.

"She's going to love it."

My mother had been trying to get me to wear more makeup ever since we got back from California.

"Just a little color on your cheeks," she would say to me.

When Emi drove me home, I ran into the house. Ajax was at the door, wagging his tail and sniffing at my knees. I was sniffing, too—fresh baked oatmeal cookies.

I could hear CNN on in the family room. In our house, the family room and the kitchen were one big room. Mom was hunkered down on family room couch, surrounded by student papers, journals, a coffee mug and the TV remote.

I peeled a cookie off the brown paper bag. "Great cookies, Mom." I shared some of it with Ajax.

"Thank you." She didn't look up.

I walked in the family room with my arms in the air. I spun around in front of her and took a bow. "What do you think of my face?" I beamed.

It was an unexpected answer.

"Mr. Owens called. He wanted to know why you weren't in school today."

CHAPTER TWO

I figured I would be grounded forty days and forty nights—no phone calls, no TV and definitely no going out. It was another milestone on my road to recovery—my first punishment since I got sick.

"Do you have anything you want to say?" Her voice was calm; it would have been better if she were yelling.

I shook my head no.

I glanced over at the TV. CNN was doing a story on the Marine Corps's new boot camp.

"Rell, we need to talk." She patted the sofa cushion, and as soon as she did, Ajax leaped up next to her.

"Get down!" She pointed to the floor.

Poor dog. He must be so confused.

"Sit, Rell."

I would have rather faced a Marine drill instructor.

"Rell, I know this year has been tough on you. It's been tough on all of us." She had a crumpled tissue clutched in her fist.

I nodded.

"Your going back to school was something we were all looking forward to."

The Marines were scaling ropes dangling from helicopters.

Mom clicked the TV off.

"I'm sorry, Mom," I started to explain.

"Let me finish." She put her hand up like a crossing guard. "Rell, I was worried about you all day long. I was glued to my pager. I checked my voice mail every ten minutes and dropped by the office twice to see if you had called." She took in a deep breath. "But, when you didn't call, I thought things were okay. And when I picked you up from school, you seemed so happy." She shook her head. "All day, I was worried sick, but then—you were okay." Her eyes were bloodshot and her mascara was gone. "Where were you, Rell?"

"McDonald's."

"McDonald's?"

"Uh-huh."

She combed her fingers through her hair and pulled it in a bunch at the back of her neck. "You spent the entire day at McDonald's?"

"Yes."

"Emi wasn't with you?"

"She didn't know anything about it." I reached down to pet Ajax. "I know it looks bad, but it was no big deal."

"It is a very big deal, Rell."

Only if you make it one, Mom.

"Rell, this kind of behavior isn't normal for you. If you weren't ready to go back to school, you should have told me." She sighed. "You know I would have understood. We could have put it off for a week or so. My God, Rell, we could have talked to Mr. Owens about extending your time at home."

"I don't need an extension."

"Rell, you didn't go to school."

"It's not like I robbed a bank, Mom." I could hear my voice getting louder.

"Rell."

"I'll go to school tomorrow," I said.

"But why didn't you go today?"

Because I didn't want to!

"I don't know."

The phone rang. Mom let it ring.

"Rell, there's more to this than just not wanting to go to school."

"No. There's not, Mom!"

"Rell, you need to deal with this."

The phone rang again.

"There is nothing to deal with." I shook my head and stared at a blank TV.

On the third ring, Mom picked up the phone. "Hello." She cupped the receiver of the phone. "It's your father," she whispered.

"No, David, she's fine. She just got back from Emi's house." Mom cleared the papers off her lap. "Why bother getting involved now?" She got up and walked into the kitchen. "I'll call. What's the number?" She flipped through the notes on the refrigerator. "Don't make promises you can't keep, David." She scribbled something down. "I told you before, I don't care." There was a pause. "Rell and I will go out." Another pause. "Fine." Mom paced between the sink and the fridge with the phone nuzzled on her shoulder. "I said, 'fine,' David." And she hung up the phone.

No "I love you," no "We'll see you later," not even a "Good-bye"—just "Fine."

Mom turned to me. "Dad's going to be late."

"I figured," I said.

Mom opened the refrigerator door. "So, we can go out to eat, or…," she leaned over and moved things around. "Have leftover stir fry."

"Do we have any frozen pizza?"

She opened the freezer and held up the box. "Mushroom and sausage."

I walked into the kitchen and stood next to the counter. "I am sorry about missing school, Mom."

"Rell, sometimes I don't think I can handle one more thing, Sweetheart."

Me neither, Mom.

Her eyes widened as she looked at me. "What's this?" She tilted my chin to the ceiling light.

"My new makeup. Emi did it," I said.

"You look beautiful."

I walked over to my purse and pulled out the Seventeen. I opened it to "Natural Makeup for Sophisticates."

"She did a great job." Mom angled the magazine to read my notes in the margin.

"She showed me how to do it too, so when I go to school, tomorrow, I can do it myself."

"Rell, I still want you to talk this out with Dr. Maitlin."

"Why?"

"Just this time, Rell."

It was always "just this time."

"Why don't you talk to her?"

"I'm swamped at school right now, Rell."

"What about Dad?"

"Dad's not the issue."

"The two of you fight all the time." I could hear myself whine.

"I already made the appointment for you."

"Can't I call her instead?"

When I was at Stanhope I called Dr. Maitlin every week. I had a hospital psychologist in San Francisco, but I liked Dr. Maitlin better. She never lied to me and she never told Mom what I said.

"She can fit you in on Thursday. I'll pick you up after school."

When I was a little kid and my mother was cold, I would have to put on a sweater. When she was tired, I had to take a nap. Now, when she got upset, I was the one who had to see the psychologist.

"Fine," I said.

I really didn't have a choice.

That night when Mom tucked me in bed, she ran her hand over my forehead. "I'm sorry I get so worried about you, Sweetheart. But, I love you, Rell."

"I love you, too, Mom."

She blew me a kiss from the door and I listened to hear her footsteps echo down the hall. When I was sure she was in the kitchen, I patted my hand on my bed and Ajax jumped up. He pawed at my quilt, making a nest, circled around twice and coiled himself snug my back. Within minutes he was snoring. But I couldn't get to sleep.

Ajax started running in his sleep. His paws were fluttering

and he was making muffled barking sounds. At nine forty-five I heard Dad come home from work. An hour later, he and Mom were still fighting.

It was after midnight when I finally fell asleep. I had a dream that I was stuck at the top of a Ferris wheel. My hands were clenched to the bar. The gondola rocked higher and faster. I screamed for help. The cotton candy man looked up at me from his stand. He stared at me and grinned.

I hated the nightmares; when I was in treatment I had them all the time. I reached over and hugged Ajax and tried to stay awake, but I must have fallen asleep because at about three o'clock a jab to my stomach woke me. Ajax must have stretched.

I got up and stuffed a towel under my door and turned on my computer. LB had emailed me "Just found these." One was a photo of Dr. Braden dressed like Elvis at the Halloween party the other was of Tess and me about a month before Tess died.

When I saw Tess's face, I flashed a vision of her sitting in her wheelchair with Mylar ribbon braided through the spokes of its wheels. Tess was my first roommate at Stanhope. She had bone cancer—she donated her left leg to it. I'm not sure if I would have liked Tess if she didn't have cancer. She bordered on weird. She wore a curly red wig with a blue sequined cap, and when she talked, she waved a glitter moon wand that sprinkled metal flecks all over our floor.

A few weeks before she died, I heard her sobbing in the middle of the night. I pretended to be asleep.

"Rell, are you awake?" she whispered from across the room.

I grunted.

"Do you think butterflies would like flying in the snow?"

"It's late, Tess," I answered.

"What if they knew they would die if they did it? Do you think they would still fly?"

"I don't know, Tess."

"Rell, I want to fly."

A week later her doctor told her that her treatment wasn't working. After her parents left, I went back into our room. Her curly red wig was in the middle of the floor and the glitter wand was broken in two.

"My doctor wants me to try another experimental treatment," she said. "It'll be my fourth."

I sat next to her bed and held her hand. It was twenty minutes before she spoke again. Then she looked over at me and said, "No more."

During the next few weeks she began to lose a lot of weight. Her voice got softer, and she stopped wearing tie-dyed scarves. In the end, she folded herself up like a butterfly and gently flew away.

Mom didn't go to Tess's funeral. She was sick that day. So, Dr. Braden drove LB and me to the funeral. On the walk up to the gravesite, he put his arm around LB and he held my hand.

It was the first time I had a friend die and only the second time I ever went to a funeral. I didn't know how to act. I knew how to act when I went to church or went to see a play, but when it came to a friend's funeral, I didn't know what to do.

Dr. Braden escorted LB and me to the reserved wooden seats under the canopy. I was sure everybody was staring at us, wondering which one of us was going to die next. I tried not to think about dying. I thought about how the ground reeked of horse manure fertilizer and how I didn't want it to rain because I would have to trudge through manure puddles to get back to the car. But then Tess's mom sat down in the front row. Her dad had to help hold her up. She sat there staring at Tess's coffin. She made me remember when I first got diagnosed and I thought I was going to die. And I remembered how sorry I felt for my parents, and how sad they would be when I died and how I felt like it was me who did something bad.

I printed out the photo of Tess and taped it to my monitor and went back to bed. Four hours later my alarm went off. Ajax stretched out his spine, head down, back arched with his tailbone in the air. Then he yawned and went back to sleep.

It must be great to be a dog.

I dragged myself into the shower, not really awake. I turned on the water, soaped up my washcloth and slid it down my chest and stomach, careful not to touch my scar. The scar went from my diaphragm to nine inches down.

I ran the cloth over my scalp. A few more weeks, I thought, and I'll be ready for shampoo.

"It's quarter after seven," Mom yelled from the kitchen.

I dried myself off, got dressed and propped the Seventeen behind the sink. Mechanically, I followed Emi's directions. I listened for her voice in my head. "Swirl and flick," she said. "Bring the color to your eyes, not your nose. Stroke. Flick. Blend. Gloss."

"It's seven-thirty, Rell." Mom turned into the town crier.

I stepped back to get a better view of my face. "Not bad," I said. "Not bad at all."

By the time I came out for breakfast, Dad had already left for work. He was leaving earlier and coming home later each week. I ate my breakfast, careful not to say or do anything that would get me in trouble. Then I packed my backpack and headed to the car.

The Kimo and Kit Show was on the radio. Life seemed a bit more normal. Mom didn't drive up the front lot at school; she pulled over at the curb.

"Do you have your cell phone with you, Rell?" Mom asked.

"Yes, Mom."

"Do you have my pager number?"

"The same one you've had for three years?"

"I'll be in the computer lab most of the day," she said. "Page me if you need me. I can leave anytime."

"I know, Mom."

"I don't have any classes today."

"I'm okay, Mom."

She leaned over and gave me a hug. "I love you, Sweetheart."

"Me, too."

I shut the door and leaned in on the window. "You don't have to stay around, Mom. I really am going in."

"I love you, Rell."

"Bye, Mom."

She waved but didn't pull away. I could feel her eyes on me as I opened the door.

I walked in.

Step one: Go to see Mr. Owens.

Mr. Owens was about forty, overweight, slightly balding, with dyed black hair and yellow teeth. He had a thick neck and a square jaw. In college he was an athlete. His shelves were lined with peeling gold trophies and very few books. Framed on his wall, next to his diploma, was a Tinman Triathlon number with a citation for placing twenty-third in his age group.

"Today will be an adjustment for you, Estrella." He sounded like he had practiced that line all morning.

"Uh-huh." I stared at the spray can of Raid and the tins of Roach-Away leaning against his windowsill.

"There are stages of accepting changes in life," he said. "Changes, um, like," he cleared his throat. "Having an illness. Um, these stages include anger, resentment and rebellion."

His office smelled like popcorn.

"Has anyone talked to you about these stages, Estrella?" He tilted a manila folder up.

I nodded.

"It is normal to rebel during these stressful times and do things you might not ordinarily do. Like cutting school, for example." He nodded at me and smiled.

There were burnt popcorn kernels on his desk. I thought that he probably dropped popcorn on the floor and never cleaned it up. No wonder he had ants and roaches.

"You may be going through one of those phases now." He kept looking down at the folder.

"When I was three I went through a phase of wetting my bed." I opened my mouth and the words flew out. Not even I could believe I said it.

Mr. Owens scribbled a note in my file. He probably wrote "Experiencing a post-bedwetting trauma."

I watched the ants marching in a single file up the wall behind his desk and out the window, and I wished I were an ant right behind them.

"Students may be curious about your appearance." He tugged at his collar. "You have lost considerable weight."

And I'm wearing a wig and I don't have eyebrows. But my makeup looks great!

"They may ask questions," he said.

Like what's the capital of North Dakota. That's always been a hard one for me.

Mr. Owens offered to schedule a sensitivity session in each of my classes.

"No, thanks," I said.

I was actually started to feel sorry for him. Having to talk to girls straight off the cancer ward probably wasn't his favorite thing to do. I tried to figure out what his favorite thing to do was and decided it was giving locker room talks about how and why to wear condoms.

Finally, he gave me an envelope of papers that needed to be filled out. Standing up, he shook my hand and wished me luck on my first day back. I thanked him, swung my backpack over my shoulder and ran down to English class.

I wasn't sure why I ran—whether it was running away from him, to my class, or just plain running to get the day over with—but I ran to English class. I was still panting when I opened the door Mr. Meyers stopped lecturing. Everyone in the room got still.

"Welcome back, Rell," Mr. Meyers said.

"Thanks," I said, and started walking sideways down the row of desks.

"Come over here." He extended his arm to me. "This is a big day for us."

As I edged over to him, Frank Vasconsales and Faye Shibuya got out of their seats, each with a lei in hand.

"Welcome back, Rell." Faye draped a ti leaf and pink rose lei over my shoulders. She kissed me and gave me a hug.

Frank shuffled behind her. "Yeah, Rell, we missed you." He almost tossed the lei of white tuberose over my head.

"Way to go, Frank." I heard from the back of the room.

I held the tuberose up to my nose and inhaled it. Its petals were slightly tinged brown.

"It looked a lot better yesterday," Frank said.

"Thanks." I stood on my tiptoes and kissed his cheek.

There was a whistle from the back of the room.

"I missed you, Rell," Paul Cruz yelled.

"Thanks, Paul."

He stood in the aisle, thrusting his fists high over his head then he took a deep bow.

"Sit down, stud man," Carole said.

Then Paul started clapping, then Carole and Diane Benitez clapped, and from somewhere, someone started to chant, "Rell, Rell, Rell!" And one by one the whole class was standing and chanting and clapping. They were clapping for me, like it was a movie, starring me, Rell DeMello.

"We are all happy to have you back," Mr. Meyers said.

The clapping started again and somehow, I didn't cry.

"Thanks. Thanks a lot." I never felt like that in my life.

When the kids settled down Mr. Meyers scanned the

room. "If you need some help catching up on things, Leilani volunteered to tutor you."

Leilani waved and threw me a kiss.

"And Wanda," Mr. Meyers pointed to where she was sitting, "kept a journal of what happened in class while you were gone."

"Waa-nn-daah," some boy sang out. "Oh, Waa-nn-daah."

"That's enough." Mr. Meyers said.

There were a few more snickers from the back.

"Settle down, people." Mr. Meyers turned toward me and quietly said, "If you want Leilani to tutor you, talk to me after school and I'll get some material together. But, if you would rather catch up on your own, I can work up a package for you to go through with your mother." He turned his attention back to the class and put his hands in the air to settle down the class.

"Thanks," I said, and I walked down the aisle to my desk, my chair, looking out my school window at my very own mountains.

"Let's get back to work," Mr. Meyers said. "Page one hundred eighty-three, Edgar Alan Poe. Rell, if you didn't bring your book, double up."

"Double up"—just like normal.

A couple of times during class I checked out what kids were wearing—new clothes, new haircuts, new couples. I read the bulletin board notices about seniors buying prom bids and deadlines for graduation tickets. Almost the whole year went by without me.

After class some guy I didn't know high-fived me, Carole had a lei for me and Jacqueline Maldonado gave me a present. The second bell rang for the next period; I headed out to the hall. But once I stepped out I got swept away into the crowd. Everybody was rushing and yelling and bumping into each other. I cradled my notebook against my chest and walked close to the wall, angling myself toward the lockers, trying to keep my back to the crowd. I was trying to protect my scar. I knew it was crazy but I was sure that if someone hit me, my scar would open and my guts would spill out, right there on the floor with the whole world of Kailua High watching.

From the middle of the rush, I heard Nate call, "Rell!"

It was easy to spot him, six foot three, spiky black hair, and the world's greatest smile.

"How's it going?" he asked.

"Great." I maneuvered myself next to him so that I could use him as a shield. "How's it with you?"

"Good."

I already ran out of conversation!

"There's a substitute teacher in math class. Did anybody tell you?" he asked.

"No." I said and stopped at Room 3-D. "This is my next class," I said.

"Mrs. Marist had some kind of surgery." He walked backwards down the hall. "She's going to be out for a month."

"See you later," I said.

"Later."

At the beginning of history class, Mr. Field welcomed me back. It took him all of thirty seconds. It was short, polite and to the point. No one in class stood up and no one gave me a lei. It was just like I had hoped for.

They could have at least clapped.

History class was a double period. The class was studying Sherman's March to the Sea, certainly a relevant topic for fifteen year olds living in Hawai'i. By ten-thirty I was getting drowsy. It was hard for me to sit still so long. I hadn't been confined to a desk for eight months and I was used to getting up and walking around whenever I felt like it. And whenever I got tired, I could curl up and take a nap.

I lifted my lei, my English class lei, to my nose and inhaled their sweetness. And I thought about Violet's Lei Shoppe on Maunakea Street. Violet's was a narrow stall. In the front was a refrigerator case of strung lei, and in the back were card tables piled with flower heads being strung together by ladies picking blossoms one-by-one and sliding them on long, thin needles.

Somewhere between Mr. Field's lecture, the lei stands and Dean Ueyhara's suck up questions, it started to rain. Three cooing doves huddled under the eaves of the roof, and I sketched them in my notebook. Then one flew away and there were only two, then the second one flew away

When I was at Stanhope I missed the mountains more than the ocean—the clouds smoking around their peaks, the waterfalls, the smell of mountain fern.

"Am I making myself clear?" Mr. Field asked the class.

I smiled at him and nodded and tried to look like I was paying attention, but every two minutes I checked the clock. I would have sworn it was going backwards. Ten, nine, eight more minutes until the bell. Three, two, one. Lunch period!

Emi met me in the hall. She offered to go through the

cafeteria line for me. I never thought I would let anyone do that for me, but I said yes, and she delivered one Diet Coke, vegetarian chili, sticky rice and a garden salad to our table.

"Sorry it took so long," Emi said. "The genius at the register couldn't make change for the soda machine."

Emi was wearing the star earrings I bought for her in San Francisco.

She put both trays down and sat in the chair across from me. "It's great to have you back, Rell." She grinned.

"Thanks."

"And your makeup looks absolutely gorgeous."

I lifted my chin. "I had it professionally applied." I laughed.

"Look at your lei." Emi reached over and held up the white ginger. "My favorite."

"You should have been in English class," I said. "Kids stood up and clapped for me. They clapped! It was like I was Miss America. Mr. Meyers was so nice. And Jacqueline Maldonado gave me a present." I pulled out a small gold foil box and opened it. It was a ceramic angel pin.

"You better put it on fast. You're going to need it." Emi stared over my shoulder. "Wanda Yamanaka is headed straight for you."

"Re-ee-el."

Only Wanda could turn my name into a three-syllable song.

"Welcome back, Rell." She kissed the top of my head.

I was sure she was testing to see if my hair was a wig.

"How are you?"

Do you really want to know, Wanda?

She brushed her hair off her face with both her hands and followed it up with a wide-mouthed smile.

"Rell, you were so swamped after English class we didn't get a chance to talk," she said.

Wanda, we never talked.

"You are back in school, aren't you?" Her voice dripped with concern. "I mean for the rest of the year?"

"Yes."

"I've been so worried about you. I asked Emi about you every day. But you know how close-mouthed she is."

I looked over at Emi, who was head down in her pizza.

"Thanks for asking about me," I said.

Then, without taking a breath, she spewed a tragedy about her car getting scratched in the Neiman Marcus parking lot, the rude the security guard, the uninterested the store manager and how her mother was canceling her Neiman's charge card.

"I'm sure Neiman's is crushed," Emi mumbled.

"You know, Rell," Wanda twined her fingers through her hair—her two-hundred-dollar-hair-cut, dyed-red, permed, Japanese hair. "I had a great idea for the school paper." She was almost cooing.

"I'm sure you think all of your ideas are great," Emi said. Wanda was oblivious.

"You could write an inspirational piece on what it was like to almost die."

Emi dropped her pizza.

"I'd rather not," I said.

"Then you could include a copy of it when you applied to colleges," Wanda said.

Not even Wanda could be this dense.

"No." It was a lot better than what I really wanted to say.

"It could get you into a better college," she said.

Out of the corner of my eye, I saw Sarah Reynolds coming toward me.

"Welcome back, Sweet Cakes." Sarah gave me a big hug.

"Rell, I had another idea." Wanda edged herself between Sarah and me. "The school paper could do a profile of you. You know, fighting cancer."

"Go for it, Rell," Emi said. "You can dress up like a sumo wrestler and fight a fat cancer cell."

"What about Joan of Arc?" Sarah said, "Now, there's a fighter."

Wanda turned to Sarah, eyeballing her from the top of her spiked hair to the tips of her blue-painted toenails. "Think about it, Rell. That kind of publicity could do you a lot of good."

I wanted to strangle her.

Sarah spun her hands in the air and pretended to sprinkle fairy dust over Wanda. "Be gone," she said.

"You are so weird." Wanda scowled.

Sarah sprinkled her again.

"Weird," Wanda said as she walked away, backwards. "Think about it," were her trailing words as she went back to her galaxy of a star of one.

"I owe you, Sarah."

Sarah rippled her fingers in the air. "A sprinkle of gold dust and the troll is gone."

"I wouldn't waste the gold," Emi said.

"Silver doesn't penetrate collagen," Sarah answered.

"That's it!" I said. "I thought her lips looked bigger."

Sarah put her index finger to her lips, mocking shooting an injection into them. "The better to gossip with, my dear."

I curled my lower lip down and thrust my tongue toward my nose.

"Good likeness," Emi said.

"Oh Rell, I missed you so much." Sarah hugged me again.

"The cards you sent me were the best," I said.

"Did you like the one of the hula dancer?"

"He was gorgeous," I said.

Sarah bent her knees, tilted her pelvis and rotated her hips. "Weren't his thighs incredible?"

"Incredible," I said. "I even taped the card to my best friend's wall, hoping it would get her to come to Hawai'i." As soon as I said it, I wanted to swallow back time, taking my words with me. Why did I say "my best friend?" Emi was my best friend. She also had excellent hearing.

I pictured my words flying across a computer screen into a file labeled "Emi's brain." I looked over to her. She wasn't registering any emotion on her face. She had her eyes fixed on Sarah.

"Anna." Sarah waved Anna Cho over to the table, but she kept walking. Sarah called her again, waving her arms higher, calling her louder.

I got up to give Anna a hug, but she moved back, not a step, or even a half step, nothing you'd really notice unless you felt it happening. "Thanks for the balloons," I said, and instead of hugging her I decided to reach for her arm. She tensed up.

"It was no big deal," Anna said.

I turned to Sarah and Emi and said, "They were in the shape of rainbows." I wanted to see if Anna even knew what they looked like.

"Cool," Anna said.

She didn't have a clue.

Emi slid her chair over to make room at the table. "You want to sit with us?" she asked.

"I can't," Anna said. "I'm sitting with Makana. You know how she gets if she has to wait. Maybe we could have lunch tomorrow."

"Sure," I said, knowing that tomorrow would never come.

Sarah picked up her books. "I've got to go, too, Love Bug. I've got a lunchtime Honor Society meeting. The new president is very intense."

"Nate Lee's the president," Emi added.

"He wants to fix everything." Sarah pumped up her biceps. "He's got real man issues."

Sarah left, then Carol came by, then Trudy and Karla and Kim. By the end of lunch I was hugged and kissed, showered with lei of candy, ribbon and crocheted yarn. I had three Mylar balloons tied to my chair and a bouquet of drooping yellow roses on the table.

Kim was first to ask me about cancer. The table got quiet and everybody looked at Emi, as if they were asking Emi if it was okay to ask.

I knew they were all curious, and I knew they were afraid to ask. The hospital psychologist said it was something like asking about a friend about getting a period before you got yours.

I tried acting like cancer was no big deal. I told the jokes I'd practiced, but I couldn't make them funny. So, I told stories about shopping for my wigs and how I could fit into a size one now instead of a seven.

"I'm so skinny that my collar bone holds up my bra." I tried to sound like a stand-up comedian.

Little by little, one nervous laugh after another, we all got more comfortable with each other. Slowly they started telling me about the rumors at school—that I had an amputated leg, a brain tumor, leukemia, and my favorite, that I had died. It was a bad case of telephone tag and I was "it."

Wanda told Karla I was dying. Karla told Kim who asked Emi if it was true.

"If Wanda thought I was dying, why didn't she send me a card?" I asked.

"She was still in surgery getting her lips done." Emi puckered up. "She wanted to look good for the funeral."

As lunch talk went on, I found out it was Emi who stopped all of the rumors.

My best friend, Emi.

After lunch Carol cleared our table of the Frito bags, soda cups, unfinished nachos, salad boxes and sushi. Karla pushed back the chairs and tables and Carol carried my books to my next class.

I was feeling tired. My back hurt and I had no energy left to keep up the smiles. But, I told myself, no matter what, smile. I had to prove to everybody that I was the same old Rell, even if I wasn't.

On the way to class I stopped by my locker and put my flowers and lei away. Even their weight felt heavy on my shoulders.

When I walked into class I remembered that Nate said we had a sub. Her name was Mrs. Cyril. She was the sub from hell.

The first thing she did was to give a pop quiz. Not only did I not know the answers, I didn't even understand the questions. I turned around to look at Nate and caught him in a half-finished yawn that broke into a wide smile. He winked at me. I winked back. It was a reflex.

After class Nate asked me how I thought I did on the quiz. "Not great," was my answer.

"She's been drilling us on that stuff all last week," he said. "No explanations and she's not the best at answering questions."

"I'm not sure an explanation would have helped me," I said.

As the two of us walked down the hall I saw some more kids I hadn't seen since September.

"You're quite the celebrity," he said.

"For today," I replied.

"Where's your next class?"

"I'm going to sit the rest of the day out in the library," I said.

"See you," he said and walked down the hall and I watched him until all I could see was his shadow around the corner.

Then I headed to the library. After school I met Emi in the parking lot. "Do you want to go to Jamba Juice?" she asked me.

"My mom is picking me up."

"Is she making sure you're not at McDonald's?" Emi asked.

"She's making sure of everything."

"What if I come by later?" Emi asked.

"I'll call you," I said. I pictured myself in bed, taking a

nap, not having to talk to a soul. "I'm kind of tired."

Mom had pulled up. "I'm sorry I'm late." She was frazzled. "There was an unexpected faculty meeting, and...."

"Hi, Mrs. DeMello." Emi waved.

Mom gave her a cursory wave.

"You're not late, Mom." I handed her my lei.

"These are gorgeous, honey." She spread them out on the back seat. "Do you want to stop somewhere on the way home?"

"I just want to go home." I got in and waved to Emi.

This time there were no questions about what I did in school that day. I pushed my seat back, closed my eyes and slept on the entire way home. And when I got home I slept until dinner, when I thought I would need all of my energy to answer Mom and Dad's questions about my first day back.

But, it was Dad, not me, who made the big announcement that night.

CHAPTER THREE

Dad's construction company bid on two jobs, one in Hilo on the Big Island, the other in Guam. All I knew about Guam was that it was hot and humid and that the brown tree snake had eaten all their birds. At first I thought we would have to move there, but Dad said if the company got that bid he would move to Guam by himself.

Mom sat with her chair angled toward me, away from Dad. She pushed her peas around her plate and left most of her chicken untouched. Before dinner she poured herself a glass of wine, then two more during dinner.

"If I go to Guam, it will most likely be for a year," Dad said.

Mom plunked her wineglass down so hard that red splashes spotted the tablecloth.

"I'd get home about one weekend a month." Dad looked at me.

"What are the chances of the Hilo job coming through?" I asked.

He answered, "fifty-fifty." They were the same odds I was giving their marriage.

For the rest of dinner my head bounced like a ping-pong ball. I talked to Mom. Mom talked to me. I talked to Dad. Dad talked to me. But neither of them talked to the other.

Right after dessert I headed into my room. I emailed LB about my first day back at school. I told her about the lei I got in English class, about Wanda at lunch and Mrs. Cyril in math. I never mentioned Dad and Mom fighting.

I thanked her for the photos of us and the one of Tess. And right before I went to bed I put more tape on the corners of her picture to keep it from curling up. When I did, I traced her face with my fingers. "I miss you," I said.

As soon as I got in bed, Ajax curled under the covers, snug against me like a puppy against its mother. I wondered what it would be like to be a puppy in a big litter, all your brothers and sisters tossing and tumbling, playing all the time and nobody ever really fighting.

I hated it when Mom and Dad fought. They didn't fight so much before I got sick.

By my second day at school, most of my friends had seen me, and I decided that things didn't go so badly. I was feeling pretty good about being back. I thought the worst was over. I thought wrong.

Enter: Mrs. Cyril.

From the minute she took attendance, I knew I was in trouble.

"Estrella DeMello," she called.

"Here." I raised my hand.

She looked up and frowned. She looked like a cross between Ichabod Crane and every fairy tale's wicked stepmother.

She walked up and down the aisles, handing out our quiz sheets. She read each student's name, then stood over them, holding the quizzes in front of them before she let go. She smiled at some students. I wasn't one of them.

When she stood next to me she said, "The average grade

on this quiz was 68 percent. The median was 75 percent. Had it not been for some incredibly low scores, the mean could have been two percentage points higher. Those of you who failed this quiz don't have the slightest idea of what I just said." She handed me my paper. "Mean, median, average—it may as well be Greek to you."

I scored a whopping 28.

"Clearly, some of you shouldn't be in this class." She spit when she spoke. "Until the class average reaches 70 percent we will have daily quizzes."

Everybody groaned.

Cyril stopped at my desk. She stared down at me and said in a voice loud enough for everybody to hear, "Estrella, perhaps you should consider getting a tutor."

I stared right back. *Screw you! I've stared down a lot worse than you.*

For the rest of class I didn't hear a word she said. I fantasized about her going to the principal to complain about me then the principal would tell her that I had cancer. He would make her apologize to me in front of the whole class and then he would fire her.

I was still ranting about her after school on the way to Coconut Joe's.

"Relax," Emi said.

I slammed the door of Emi's car. "She is such a bitch." I threw my books on the back seat. "Who does she think she is?" I yanked the seat belt across my chest. "She's a lousy sub!"

Emi kept driving.

"She probably can't get a real teaching job," I said.

"I heard that the first ten times you said it."

"Can we get rid of this Hawaiian music?" I punched button after button on the car radio—news, jazz, commercials. I settled on the oldies station.

"Is anything else bothering you?" Emi looked over. She raised her eyebrows. "Does the princess want the air conditioning off? Windows down? How about a pillow for her royal ass?"

"She's a sub," I said. "A shitty low-life sub." I was repeating myself, just like my mother did.

Emi pulled in to Coconut Joe's parking lot. She spotted some college guys at a table outside. "Check them out," she said.

There were some older guys in Pacific University T-shirts huddled around a table crammed with laptops, books, coffee and cigarettes.

Emi walked directly in front of their table. She walked slower than usual, holding herself taller, not looking at them, but laughing about Cyril in that loud, fake, drama-class kind of way.

"I wish I could transfer to a different high school," I said.

She turned to me, and hardly moving her lips, she said, "Let's not advertise the fact that we're in high school, okay?"

"Who cares?" I said.

"I care." She had a phony smile plastered on her face. She looked ridiculous with that grin.

"Grab that table next to them." She poked me in the ribs. When she did, I shot my arm over my scar to protect it. "They're smoking," I said.

Emi flipped her hair off her shoulders and smiled. "Just do it."

"No." I followed her in the door and ordered my own drink.

When we came out the table next to the guys was still empty. Emi, not by accident, sat in the chair facing them.

"I don't know what her problem is." I dragged my chair out.

"They're looking at us," Emi said.

"What a bitch! Lousy sub."

"Everyone here already knows that, Rell." Emi smiled at the guys and shrugged her shoulders.

"I bet she's been a sub her whole life. She probably doesn't have a life," I said.

Emi leaned over and dug her fingers into my forearm. "Rell, if you don't stop, they'll leave."

"Does she care that I've been poisoned, radiated and cut wide open?"

"Not so loud."

"I almost died."

"You didn't almost die."

"Well, I almost-almost died."

"No points for almost," Emi said.

"I'm bald. Do I get points for that?" I ripped the paper wrapper off my straw.

"You're scaring them away." Emi never let go of her smile.

The guys closed their laptops and collected their stuff.

"See what you've done."

One of them shook his head as he walked away.

"Emi, they're college guys. They know we're fifteen year old virgins who wouldn't know what to do if they asked us out."

"Well, they do now—Miss Virgin, I-almost-died." Emi

clutched her throat. "I was cut open, tortured and I'm bald."

"I'm sorry." I shrugged.

"Too late."

"What if I dance naked on the table? Will you forgive me then?" I said.

"Twirling your wig in the air," she added.

"Deal," I said.

"Rell, you should take it off in math class. Picture it. You hurl your wig at her. Cyril screams. She clutches her heart. She falls to the floor gasping for breath. You're the only one who knows CPR. She begs you to help her. And with her dying breath she screams, 'Forgive me, Estrella.'"

"Good fantasy—five stars." I poked my straw into my mango shake. "But she's still a bitch."

"Lighten up, Rell." I crunched up my face. The best I could do was a smirk.

"Come on, Rell, even cancer patients are allowed to laugh."

She had no right to say what cancer patients could do.

Emi pulled herself up closer to the table. "Don't get mad at me, Rell, but maybe Cyril is right."

"What?" I could feel my blood surge to my face.

"If you got a tutor it would get Cyril off your back and you could catch up faster."

"I don't need a tutor."

"You're flunking math."

"I'm not flunking."

"28 must be passing in your world."

I hated it when Emi was right.

"Sarah could tutor you," she said.

"She's too busy."

"Maybe she could match you up with somebody from the National Honor Society?"

"Right. Some social zero with a computer he calls 'Honey Girl.'"

"You never know. He might turn out to be a hula dancer with incredible thighs?"

There it was. She heard the remark about the dancer's thighs. That meant she heard me call LB my "best friend."

I felt like a sleazy soap opera husband who was in love with two different women. And in a weird way, I understood him. I had two best friends: Emi, who was my best friend for life, and LB, who was fighting for her life.

The next day at school, Nate stopped at our table.

"Hey, Rell, you have minute?" he said.

"Rell and I are having lunch alone today," Emi said without giving me a chance to answer him.

"It's about math class," he said.

I handed my soda cup to Emi. "Would you mind filling this for me?" I gritted my teeth into a frozen smile and bulged my eyes out as if to say, "Do not blow this for me!"

With a grand sweep of her hand, she snatched up the cup but she didn't budge.

Nate put his foot up on the chair next to me and rested his cafeteria tray on his knee. He had on a maroon Year of the Dragon T-shirt. He looked over at Emi.

"Emi. My soda?" I kept the smile pasted on my face.

"Anything for you." She glared at Nate and walked away.

Nate looked down at his tray, then, almost stuttering he said, "Rell, I've got a 97 average in math."

"Is that a 97 average or a 97 mean?" I smirked.

"Average." He smiled. "So, if you want help," he paused. "Well, if you want a tutor…." His voice trailed off.

"So the class average can hit 70?" I asked.

"And no more daily quizzes?" He laughed, and when he did I could imagine what he looked like when he was in second grade. He probably had the same smile he did then.

"I'm a good tutor, Rell."

In the middle of the cafeteria, with everyone watching, a cute junior boy was asking me if I wanted him to tutor m.

"I wouldn't charge you anything," he said.

Be cool. Just breathe. Don't tell him yes right away.

"Let me think about it," I said. My heartbeat was throbbing so loud I could hardly hear my own words. Let me think about it? Did I really say that?

"I know how it is to miss a lot of school," Nate said.

I nodded. "Emi told me your grandfather died. I'm sorry."

Nate looked puzzled. "He died three years ago."

Emi was back in record time. "Still here, Nate?"

"It looks like it," he said.

"Well, you can leave now. We're having lunch alone."

Nate looked at me. I smiled. "See you in class."

"In class," he repeated and picked up his tray.

"Nate." I pointed to his Year of the Dragon T-shirt. The dragon was deep green with flaming breath that curled through daggers and smoke. "Were you born in the Year of the Dragon?"

"No. Year of the Tiger. We're fearless, gallant and smart,"

he said walking away.

"Fearless, gallant and smart," Emi mocked. "He forgot conceited, arrogant and pushy."

"You're not being fair," I said.

Emi cocked her head and fluttered her eyelashes. "Were you born in the Year of the Dragon?"

"What is it with you and him? Do you two have a history I don't know about?"

"Me and Tiger Boy? I don't think so."

"Well, what then?"

"I don't know. I don't trust him."

"He offered to tutor me in math." I dug my spoon into my chili.

"You don't know anything about him."

"Right. He's a serial killer masquerading as the honor society president."

"He's a social zero. There's no masquerading that."

"I'm going to say yes." I licked the chili off my spoon.

"I thought you were going to ask Sarah to find you a tutor."

"I did. She said Nate was the best tutor in school."

"What does she know?" Emi picked the onions off her burger.

During the rest of lunch I fantasized about what it would be like to have Nate as a tutor. I pictured the two of us studying in the library where everyone would see us, leaning into each other over our books, the two of us at my house when no one was home.

During math I pictured him riding a surfboard in flower print baggies, playing basketball in a torn T-shirt and gray sweats, running at the beach with Ajax and me. A few times during class I stretched out my neck and faked a yawn, turning to the back of the room to catch a glimpse of him. He was taking notes on what Cyril was saying; he never looked up.

After math class Nate came down my aisle and leaned on the desk next to mine. "Did you think about it?" he asked.

"I did." I tried to sound coy.

"And?"

"You've got a deal."

"When do you want to start?" he asked.

"I don't know."

"How about three-thirty? I'll meet you in the parking lot," he said.

"You mean today?"

"Exactly."

"Wow, you work fast," I said. "I can't today, I have an appointment after school. What about tomorrow?"

"Great. Three-thirty on the soccer field side of the parking lot." He announced it like it was a binding contract.

I wondered if he would ask me to the prom.

This is crazy. You talked to the guy a total of three times and one of those times was a 'Hi' in the mall parking lot. He's a junior. He wants to be your tutor. That's all there's to it.

After school that day, on the ride over to Dr. Maitlin's, I pretended to be asleep in the car. I couldn't stop thinking about Nate. I wondered if I should tell Dr. Maitlin about him, even though there was nothing to tell. I decided not to say anything. It was a dumb idea, and besides, I didn't want to jinx anything before it happened.

I wondered if I should act dumb at first, so he would think he's a great tutor. I wondered if I should smile a lot or look serious, look in his eyes or twirl my pencil. Everything was a life shaping decision—red jumper? jeans? perfume or not? *Get a grip, Rell.*

By time we got to the hospital parking lot I had decided to wear my red, hoop earrings and lemongrass cologne—not too sweet with a right amount of tang.

When Mom let me off at the East Wing door, she recited all her errands she would do while I was with Dr. Maitlin and she asked me if she could pick up anything from the health food store, just like she always did. Then she assured me she would be waiting for me in the exact spot in exactly one hour. She ended with, "I love you, Rell."

I recited my answers back to her. "I love you, too Mom. I'll wait for you right here if you're late and I don't want anything special from the health food store."

I walked in the hospital and got in the elevator. I checked myself out in the smoked glass wall. I walked down to Dr. Maitlin's office. It was a long hallway of doctor's offices—all specialists—and I knew what every specialty was.

There was a cardiologist, like Dr. Greenberg who shoved pipe-sized tubes in my veins to check my heart for damage from chemotherapy. And the pulmonary specialists who measured the diminished capacity of my lungs. The gynecologist, like Dr. Rodrigues who held my hand when she told me I may, or may not be able to have children, and there was no way to test for it either.

Next door to Dr. Maitlin's office was a pediatric oncologist who treated kids for cancer. Just catching a glimpse of a bald-headed kid made me feel like I was back at Stanhope. Part of me wanted to hide the fact I that I ever had cancer. Dr.

Maitlin told me that kind of thinking was normal.

Dr. Maitlin was about fifty, blonde and athletic looking. She drove a yellow Saab convertible to work on weekdays and on weekends she rode horses. She always sat up straight. Her blouses were starched and she smelled of expensive perfume. My appointments with her always started out the same. At first we would talk about nothing. She would ask me how things were going and I would say, "Fine." It would go on like that until she figured out what I wanted to talk about.

"You went back to school this week?" Dr. Maitlin asked.

"Yes."

"How did it go?" she asked.

"It wasn't bad." I looked over at her collection of plastic dinosaurs and monsters and wondered what kind of monsters kids really attacked in her room.

"Did anybody say anything that made you uncomfortable?"

"No, it wasn't like that. Some kids got nervous around me and didn't know how to act."

"And?"

"English class was good. It was my first class. Kids stood up and clapped for me and they gave me lei."

"How did that make you feel?" she said.

"Like I deserved it."

"Deserved it how?" Dr. Maitlin crossed her legs. She kept an open notebook on her lap.

"It was like what I thought it would be when I left Stanhope. I thought all the doctors and nurses would line up along the hall and clap and hug me when I walked by, like it was a graduation."

"What did happen when you left?"

"Nobody lined up. I went to see Nick. I told you about him, right?"

"Yes," she said. "And he died the next week."

"Two weeks later," I said.

"What else happened?"

"Right before I left I said goodbye to LB. A few nurses came in and Dr. Braden was there. He had already talked to Mom and me about my follow-ups the day before. I hugged LB and that was it."

I looked at the clock. I had twenty minutes left in the session.

Dr. Maitlin pointed her toes toward her knees. Whenever she did that I knew that she was going to ask me a tough question. "Your mother called me Monday night," she said.

I rolled my eyes. "I know."

"She was upset about your cutting school."

"She's always upset." I said. "It was no big deal."

"She's worried about you."

I threw my head back on the chair. "That's all she does is worry. She asks me a million times a day if I feel okay or if I'm tired or if I'm hungry. Last week she even wanted to feel my neck where the cancer used to be." I felt the tears building in my eyes. I yanked a tissue out of the box.

Dr. Maitlin listened.

"She's always doing stuff like that. Once I caught her watching me sleep. I was in bed and woke up and I saw her standing at my door. She was watching me sleep."

Dr. Maitlin pushed her eyeglasses to the bridge of her nose.

"I feel like I'm some kind of cancer bomb, ready to go off."

She took some papers out of an envelope and handed them to me. "Your mother sent me a schedule of your check-ups."

I yanked them away from her. "This is my personal stuff," I said.

"She wanted me to be aware of those times that might be stressful for you," she said.

"She had no right to give this to you."

"It's her way of taking care of you, Rell."

"She can't do this!" I flipped the pages, reading through Mom's notes. "I have every one of these dates on my wall calendar. She knows that."

"Sometimes it's hard for parents to stop actively fighting cancer," she said.

"Then she should get her own cancer to fight." And as soon as I said it I was sorry. "I didn't mean it," I said. "But she treats me like such a baby."

"Your mother sees you as her baby."

"I'm fifteen," I said. "Girls my age have babies, and I still have to ask permission to go to the mall. All my mother thinks about is cancer. Every time she looks at me, I know she's thinking 'cancer.'" I wiped my cheek with my hand. "I hate it."

"If you had a choice, what would you want her to do?" Dr. Maitlin asked.

"I want her to forget I ever had cancer."

"Can you?"

I looked up at her. "That's unfair."

"By whose rules?"

I leaned back in the chair, tearing my tissue into threads. I wasn't going to answer that question.

Dr. Maitlin waited for awhile then asked me, "How's your

friend, Emi?"

"Okay," I said.

"Have you been doing anything together lately?"

"Not really."

She asked me about school, homework. She even asked about Ajax, but I was finished talking.

At the end of my appointment I stood up, shoved my tissues in my backpack and walked toward the door. My hand was on the doorknob when I turned around and said, "I think my parents might get divorced." I checked Dr. Maitlin's reaction. There was none.

"They fight all the time and it's always about me," I said.

She took off her glasses. "We'll talk about this next time, Rell—at the beginning of the session."

CHAPTER FOUR

By my second week back at school I started to feel like I belonged. Most kids didn't even notice me anymore. I was beginning to feel normal, although there were kids who reminded me that I wasn't.

There were the "well-wishers" who told me about every cancer survivor doing every great thing there was to do. Survivors who won the Tour de France, played professional hockey or owned billion-dollar Internet companies.

I didn't care. I wanted to meet the one survivor who could say, "I'm cured," without crossing her fingers or holding her breath. The one who wasn't afraid in the middle of the night.

Some kids at school called me heroic or brave. I wasn't heroic. Heroes have choices. I wasn't brave either. When the chemotherapy nurse walked in my room I cried before she even touched me. And after she left, I cried more.

The chemo drugs didn't care if I cried. They either worked or they didn't.

When Dr. Braden told me, "You have cancer," I cried.

When my treatment was over, he never said, "You don't have cancer anymore." He said, "I find no evidence of cancer."

"No evidence"—like weeds in a garden, creeping under the surface, until one day a pale green shoot pops through the ground and chokes the blossoming flowers.

I hated cancer. I hated the word.

At school, a girl I didn't even know came up to me and told me she read a book called *The Summer of My Tears* about a blonde cheerleader who got cancer in April, almost died in June, was cured in August, and in November was crowned Homecoming Queen at Thanksgiving. It sounded just like my life except for the part about being blonde, a cheerleader, Homecoming Queen and cured.

I wanted to ask if the book described how your hair falls out in clumps overnight and you find it on your sheets and pillow. But I could tell she wanted polite answers, not too scary and not too close.

I wasn't brave and I wasn't heroic. There were times I was angry and mean. Once in Spanish class I made a list of all the people I knew who should have got cancer instead of me.

Kids would ask me, "How could you tell you had cancer?" I wanted to tell them that one morning I was taking a shower and I felt a small boob growing out of the side of my neck and when the surgeons cut it out they found it full of cancer.

Some kids would nod like they understood, like they could line up my answers against their lives and convince themselves that it could never happen to them.

Cancer can only happen to somebody else.

But I knew it was exactly what I did myself. At Stanhope whenever somebody died I would convince myself that their cancer was different from mine, that they never did well in treatment, that their doctors weren't as good as mine.

All I wanted was to be me, Rell before cancer, not me, the girl with cancer.

My life was divided into two parts: "before" and "after" I had cancer. Before I got sick, before Mom and Dad fought, before Tess's funeral, before the nightmares.

The nightmares came with chemo—at least they did for me. When I was in treatment, sometimes I slept with the TV on or with a CD playing, to try to trick the nightmares away.

The week after Tess died I had a nightmare about fairies and thieves and a red-haired girl who thought she could sing. The girl stood in the ocean and asked the wind to carry her song. But when she opened her mouth, her voice sounded like a rusted harp—sharp and off-key and brittle from lack of use.

I woke up screaming. LB called the night nurse who toweled my face and changed my sheets, then made notes in my medical chart. LB pulled a chair over next to my bed and she slept bundled under an afghan in a chair—just an arm's length away.

But that's not what the kids at school wanted to hear. They wanted a fairy tale. "Once upon a time Estrella DeMello had cancer, and she lived happily after," like a longhaired princess rescued by a prince.

The closest I had to a prince in my life was Nate Lee. He didn't ride into my life on a white stallion, he drove up in a beat-up green pickup truck with split vinyl seats and a rusted out floor. And he never whisked me away to his castle. He took me to half-priced movies, free nights at the zoo and the Waikiki Bowl-A-Rama.

Nate was my prince. He was under-romantic and over-logical. But he did have beautiful hands.

The first time Nate tutored me I noticed his hands. He waved them through the air like an orchestra conductor. He chopped the air to make a point.

He was explaining how to calculate a median when I asked him, "Do you play the piano?"

"Why?" he asked. "Is there a way to explain median using piano keys?"

"I don't know." I laughed. "I was looking at your hands and I wondered if you played the piano."

"You and my grandmother." He formed an X with his hands and backed away from me.

"Is she that bad?" I asked.

"My San Francisco grandmother tried to turn me into a musical prodigy. She's straight out of The Joy Luck Club. 'Na-than, you be good piano play-ah.' I think she bribed the fortune teller to tell my parents that music was my destiny."

"Did you play?" I asked.

"Did I have a choice? My grandmother paid for a year of piano lessons for me. Then she came to Hawai'i for my first recital. After she heard me play, she gave up."

"Were you that bad?"

"Not only was I bad, but I was an ungrateful child, and all of China was ashamed."

"Sounds serious."

"She's still disappointed."

Nate and I studied every afternoon after school. Sometimes we met in the library, sometimes in Maui Taco, twice we went to the movies afterwards. After two weeks of Nate tutoring me, Dad referred to him as my "boyfriend," and after three weeks, Wanda Yamanaka declared us a couple. I would have voted us Couple of the Year except for one small problem—after four weeks of being together, he still hadn't kissed me.

Each night LB emailed me the same question: "Did he kiss you yet?" And each night my answer would be the same: "I'm working on it."

I wondered if he were gay, or if he really just was my tutor. Then, finally one night at the beach, he kissed me. As soon as I got home I emailed LB.

"Nate kissed me!" I wrote. "We went to the beach to look at the moon and he stood behind me. Then he put his arm around me and kissed the back of my neck."

Plink. Plink. It was incoming mail.

"What are you doing up?" I wrote. It was past midnight in California.

"Planning our Grand Canyon trip," she wrote. "But forget the Grand Canyon, tell me about tonight."

"It was great. We were standing there. I had my back to him, looking at the ocean, then he kissed me."

"Rell?" Mom knocked on the door.

I cleared my computer screen before I said, "Come in."

"Did you have a good time tonight, Sweetheart?"

"Uh-huh."

"Dad and I thought you would come home earlier," she said.

"It's not even ten o'clock, Mom."

"I know. But make sure you don't stay up too late." She

walked over to my desk and kissed the top of my head. Her hair smelled like herbal shampoo. "Writing to LB?" she asked.

"Uh-huh."

"Tell her I send her my love." Mom paused like she was going to say something, but then stopped. When she was at the door she turned and said, "Rell, are you going anywhere in the morning?"

"Emi wants to go shopping. The Sassafras Shop is going out of business."

"Before you go out, Dad and I want to talk to you."

"Did Dr. Braden call?"

"No. No doctor called. Nothing like that," she said.

Just the mention of "having a talk" and I was sure I relapsed—the cancer was back. "You want to tell me now?" I asked.

"We'll talk in the morning." She tugged at the belt of her robe before she shut the door. "It's not important." She threw me a kiss. "I love you."

"I love you, too, Mom." Although right that minute I was wondering what she was thinking.

"My mom was just in here." I wrote. "Something's up."

"Focus, Rell! This is about kissing."

"Okay. Okay," I wrote. "I knew Nate wanted to kiss me all night long. Or I was hoping he did. I caught him staring at me in the library when I was taking notes. He watched me when I walked to the water fountain. I craned my neck back to sneak a peek at him and he was watching me drink! Then, at Tropical Freeze, he was watching me lick my ice cream cone. That's when he asked if I wanted to go to the beach."

"And?" LB wrote.

"We were walking close, but not touching. Nate had his hands in his pockets. Then he put his arm around me and kind of froze like he was waiting for me to say something, but I didn't. We walked the beach for a little, then we stopped and that's when he kissed me."

"More," LB wrote.

"There is no more," I answered.

"Is he a good kisser?"

"Yes."

"Open mouth or closed?" LB asked.

"Open."

"Oh my God, I can feel his lips right now."

LB wanted to know every detail. We talked longer about that one kiss than it took for the entire date. Then we switched to talking about our trip.

"I rub my fire agate every night before I go to sleep. I can't wait to go," she wrote.

LB's fire agate was a copper-colored stone flecked with streaks of gold. Her parents bought it for her when they took her brother to the Grand Canyon while LB was in treatment.

"I found a three-day llama trek of the canyon," she wrote. "It costs two thousand dollars and you sleep in tents."

"Llamas spit. Besides, it's about fifteen hundred dollars more than I have."

"The tour company is looking for junior photographers to take action shots during the trip. Then they sell the photos to the rich tourists."

"It sounds like a spoof of the Discovery Channel."

"Will you think about it?"

"I don't know how to take pictures," I wrote.

"They teach you."

"I guess," I wrote.

"Good, because I already sent for the applications and had one sent to your house."

"My mom will love that," I wrote.

"How is your mom?"

"If she could, she'd be taking my vitals and drawing blood every three hours."

"Speaking of blood, the vampire techs send their love. They paid me a visit about an hour ago."

I knew late night visits to draw blood weren't routine. "Why are you getting your blood tested at night?" I asked.

"My counts have been low and Doc Lynch is being careful."

"Are you still getting treatments?"

"Yes."

Blood counts ruled the lives of chemo patients. If counts were too high, or too low, treatment might be postponed. And, as much as I hated getting chemo, I panicked when one of my sessions was postponed, because without treatment I was sure the cells would instantly grow back.

"Is Dr. Lynch worried about you?" I asked.

"He didn't say anything."

"What about Dr. Braden?"

"No."

"Are your parents there?" I asked.

"No. My brother is sick so my mom couldn't come and

my dad got a chance for some overtime so he's working."

"Have you had any nose bleeds?" I asked.

"No."

"Fever?"

"No."

"Rashes?"

"No rashes."

"How's your weight?"

"Stop it," LB wrote. "You're beginning to sound like a zit-faced intern."

"Sorry."

Stanhope was a teaching hospital. That meant that every few weeks another crop of terrified interns rotated through our floor, asking us the same questions as every other batch asked.

"Rell, the night nurse just came in. She had one of those are-you-still-in-here looks on her face. I better go."

"I love you, LB," I wrote.

"Right back at you, Rell."

I slid into bed and fell asleep.

The next morning I was coaxed awake by the smell of one of Dad's Saturday morning breakfasts: cinnamon pancakes, scrambled eggs, bacon and freshly squeezed orange juice.

There was a place setting waiting for me at the table. Dad was pouring Mom a cup of coffee. She put down the morning paper and thanked him. They seemed to be getting along. I leaned over and gave Mom a kiss.

"Emi called about twenty minutes ago," she said. "She's going to pick you up at nine-thirty. She said she wants to be at The Sassafras Shop when the doors open

I checked the kitchen clock. It was nine o'clock. Then I pulled the chair out next to Mom's and sat leaning forward, petting the dog and letting him lick my face. "Good boy, Ajax."

"Rell, I told you not to…," Mom started to say.

"Let the dog lick your face." I finished her sentence in a mock singsong tone. "I could get rabies, or worse yet, doggie cancer."

"That's not funny, Rell."

"It is funny, Mom." I got up and headed to the kitchen.

"Dogs carry diseases," she said.

I poured myself some juice. "It's okay, Mom, I read about a new vaccine for dog cancer."

"How is my Estrella this morning?" Dad lifted his pancake spatula high over my head and gave me a hug.

"Just wonderful, Dad."

"What can I get you? Two pancakes or three? Bacon or sausage? Bagel or toast?"

"Two pancakes with a side order of bacon and no eggs, no toast."

"David, talk to her." Mom lowered the paper and turned toward the kitchen.

"What would you like to discuss, the pressure per square inch of the concrete we're pouring at the job site?"

I wrinkled my nose. "Not on my need-to-know list, Dad."

Mom snapped the newspaper shut. "Damn it, David. This is what I was talking about. You get to be the good guy and I'm always the monster."

"Let's not start off the day like this, Maria," Dad said.

"No, let's pretend everything is wonderful."

"It is, Mom."

"Tell her, David," Mom said.

Dad turned down the stove and put the spatula down. "Your mother read about a veterinarian who quit taking care of dogs because he had Hodgkin's disease."

"So?"

"Having a dog may be a serious health risk for you." He sounded apologetic.

"You must be kidding?" I turned to Mom.

"Rell, you have to be aware of the risks?" Mom said.

"I cannot believe this." I looked to Dad for help.

"Hear your mother out on this, Rell," he said.

I threw my hands up in the air.

"Dogs carry a virus," she said. "It's the virus that's the concern. It can kill you," Mom said.

"Bacon can kill me. Eggs can kill me."

"Rell, you don't know what having a dog in the house, letting him sleep with you, having him lick you could do. You don't know what you're risking," Mom said.

"And what do you think your smoking does to me?"

Her face blanched.

Dad snapped, "Do not speak to your mother like that, young lady."

Dad just switched sides.

"I was talking about the dog," I said. "At night Ajax sneaks cigarettes in the garage like nobody's supposed to know what he's doing."

"That's enough." Dad pointed his finger toward my face.

"You apologize to your mother, right now."

"I'm sorry." I cocked my head and stared out the window.

"That was a half-ass apology if I ever heard one," Dad said. "Try again."

"I'm sorry." I said it with enough remorse to keep myself out of trouble.

Mom's voice was quiet. "The article said that dogs carry a virus that could be fatal to cancer patients, particularly Hodgkin's disease patients."

"Can I call up Dr. Braden and ask him?" I said.

"I already did," she said.

"What did he say?"

"I left a message for him, and certainly we won't do anything until we talk to him."

"What does 'do anything' mean?" I asked. "Are you getting rid of Ajax?" My eyes fixed on Dad.

"Not exactly," Mom said.

"Well, what exactly?" I glared at Mom.

"We don't know yet," Mom said.

"I'm not the boy in the space suit, Mom. I had cancer," I screamed it loud enough for the whole neighborhood to hear one more DeMello fight.

"Rell." Dad put his hand on my shoulder.

"Leave me alone." I jerked away.

"We only want what's best for you," Dad said.

Only the best for your little Estrella.

"You can't protect me forever." I was panting.

"What if Dr. Braden says it's dangerous for you to have a dog?" Mom said.

"That's crazy," I said.

"What if he does?"

"I talked about Ajax all the time," I said. "He saw pictures of him on my wall. Don't you think he would have said something?" Ajax was circling my feet. "Do you think I'm the first Hodgkin's patient in history to have a dog?" I picked him up and held him close and let him nibble on my ear and lick my face. "I am not going to die because the dog kisses me."

"Can you please put him down?" Mom asked.

"No."

"Please, Rell."

No. Not this time. I am not giving in.

I looked at Dad. "If I go out with Emi will Ajax be here when I get back?"

"Of course, he will," Dad said.

"Mom?"

"The dog will still be here," she said.

"Fine." I carried Ajax to my room and slammed the door. I let him down on the bed.

"Dog virus." I pet Ajax. "She has officially gone crazy."

Ajax licked my face.

Why can't things go back to the way they were?

I got up, turned the shower on full blast and cried. Then I got dressed, put on my makeup and marched myself through the kitchen, right out the front door without as much as telling either of them goodbye. Then I paced up and down the driveway until Emi pulled up.

I dove into her car. I tossed my purse on the floor next to a crumpled Taco Bell bag and the latest issue of *Celebrity*

Secrets.

"They've lost it!" I said. "It's like aliens have taken over their minds!" I pulled the seat belt out, but it jammed half way across my chest. "Stupid thing!" I pulled it out again.

"I assume we are talking about your parents." Emi reached over and gently tugged on the belt.

"They have absolutely lost their minds," I said locking my seat belt.

Emi glanced over her shoulder as she backed out of the driveway. "What happened?"

"They think the dog can kill me," I said.

"Biting or barking?"

"They think I can get sick from the dog licking me," I said.

Emi had braided one plait in her hair from her temple to her shoulder. There was an apple-green ribbon running through it. "Can you?" she asked.

"How can you even ask me that?"

"Simple," she said. "I don't know." She turned down Hibiscus Lane.

"I'm sure the doctors would have told me if I couldn't have a dog."

"Did they tell you other things you couldn't do?" When she turned her head her braid swung back on her shoulder.

"No drinking, no ear piercing, no tattoos, no contact sports, no drugs, blah, blah, blah."

"But, they didn't mention dogs?" Emi asked.

"No."

"So you can figure that having a dog is okay." Her face was unsmiling.

"But, they're talking about getting rid of him," I said.

"Did they say they were getting rid of him?" she asked.

I felt like a third grader being questioned by the school principal.

"No."

"Did your doctor know you had a dog?"

"Yes."

Forget the principal, I felt like Emi was a hard-nosed district attorney.

"Then can we go to The Sassafras Shop in peace now?" Emi said.

"Yes."

Emi voice was calm. "Rell, you know they won't get rid of the dog."

No, I don't know that. But, I said, "You're right," even though I didn't believe it. Then I said, "Nice ribbon," even though I didn't believe that either.

"I was thinking of getting an Indian silk cord to braid through it. Sarah told me all the Indian stuff was 75 percent off."

We turned down Ilima Road, toward Jefferson Park. As we got closer to the park, vans lined the street and there were families unloading coolers and beach chairs. A couple of boys in Little League uniforms swung their bats as they waited.

"Great dog!" Emi pointed to a Great Dane pup with surgical-tape peaked ears.

"I wonder if he'll give his family cancer," I said.

"I thought we were finished with cancer today," Emi said.

"Sorry. I didn't know it was such an issue."

Emi tapped on the steering wheel like she was sending Morse code. "It's a never-ending issue with you."

"You're right. It is never-ending."

"Look, Rell, all I want to do is to go to The Sassafras Shop. I want to buy some ribbon, try on a few toe rings and look at the dragonfly pins, and I don't want to hear about cancer. I want one day without hearing the word."

I decided that her braid looked stupid and it made her ears stick out like sugar bowl handles.

"Can't we just go shopping like we used to?" Emi looked over at me. "I drag you around, you complain, then we get something to eat." She smiled.

She shouldn't be wearing a gray top, either. It makes her skin look drab.

"Sure," I said. I looked out the window toward the narrow gulch between the cliffs. "I wouldn't want to spoil your day," I muttered.

"What now?" Emi said. Her voice was tinged with restraint.

"I said, 'I wouldn't want to spoil your day.'"

Emi sped up the hill, passing a truck with anger that was probably meant for me. "Is it so awful for me to want one day without cancer, Rell?" She swerved down Marsh Road.

"My mother says, 'Wanting is good. It builds character.'"

"I don't want to fight, Rell."

"Are we fighting?"

"Yes, we are fighting," she said.

"Okay. You want a day without cancer? I'd like a whole life without it. Do you think you can arrange that?"

"Forget I said anything, Rell."

I wouldn't stop. "Of all the people I know, I thought you would understand me."

Emi jammed on the brakes and swerved into the Yum Yum Tree parking lot and screeched into the first parking space. "Rell, you have no idea what it's like to be anybody but you. Your dog. Your hair. Your parents. Your damn cancer."

"Your clothes, your movie stars, your newest boyfriend?" I said.

"It's all you talk about. It pissed me off."

"I got cancer on purpose—just to piss you off."

Emi turned off the engine. "You don't have cancer anymore, Rell."

"You can never not have cancer anymore. You still don't know anything about it."

"I know every damn detail of it. Let me see, what don't I know?" Emi counted on her fingers. "There's the chemo drips, the radiation burns, the dry mouth, the rashes, the nightmares and night sweats. I even know that your damn pubic hairs itched when they grew back in." She shook her head. "Did I miss anything, Rell? Because if I did, it's not because you didn't tell me—every damn little detail over and over again."

"Are you through?" I asked.

"No, I'm not." Tears dripped down Emi's cheek. "I'm sick of you wearing that wig like some kind of damn merit badge."

"You're jealous," I said.

"Of what?"

"The attention I get."

"You've uncovered the truth! I want cancer, so I can have my own pity party."

"It's true."

"God, you are so self-centered." She slammed her fists on the steering wheel. "Tell me *one* thing that happened to me while you were at Stanhope."

I couldn't answer right away.

"Let me tell you. First of all, I tried out for the volleyball team. I didn't make the team. I made it to the next to the last cut, but then they picked Sharlene instead. I emailed you about it but you never bothered to mention it."

"Excuse me, I was busy fighting or my life," I said.

"Rell, the Cancer Queen …" Her voice cracked. "…was too busy to remember my birthday."

I blurted out, "I was sick." Then there was a quiet. Emi didn't say anything "Emi, you're my best friend."

"I'm your only friend."

"What's that supposed to mean?'

"The only one who will tell you the truth."

"With friends like you, who needs enemies?"

"Great response, Rell. Did you remember that from sixth grade?"

"I don't want friends who don't understand what I'm going through," I said.

"That's it! I hereby resign from the Poor-Little-Rell Club."

It was like we crossed a bridge and there was no turning back.

I was hurt and angry and I knew I was wrong, but I couldn't admit it, so I attacked instead. "Nate cares about me," I said.

"I was waiting for that," she said.

"He cares about me with or without cancer."

"He feels sorry for you."

"You're mad because I have a boyfriend and you don't."

"Right, I'm just dying to be with your tight-assed boyfriend."

I ran out of words. We both cried. Neither of us talked. A couple parked their station wagon next to us, almost banging Emi's car getting their baby out of the back seat.

"Rell, do you remember when you would call me from Stanhope and we'd talk about all the things we were going to do when you got back home?"

I nodded.

"I thought we were going to do them," she said.

"Me, too," I said.

The parents loaded the baby in his stroller and packed it with a diaper bag and toys.

"Emi, I wish I could make things go back to like they were before. But nothing will go back." I held back from really crying. "I'm really sorry if I've been a jerk."

Emi looked up and smiled. She lifted her hand and bent her pinky. "Can we go back to being best friends?"

I hooked my pinky to Emi's. "Friends forever."

We both dried off our tears.

"I didn't mean to forget your birthday," I said. "I meant to get you something. I even looked at a bear in the hospital gift shop. Honest."

"Let's just forget it," Emi said. "Or...." Emi perked up. "I'll let you buy me a toe ring at The Sassafras Shop."

"I'm not going shopping. I'll just go home. Do you mind?"

"I guess not." She seemed upset.

"I really am tired," I said and I opened the door with as little notice as I could and was getting out of the car when Emi asked, "Where are you going?"

"I'm going to walk," I said.

"Rell, it's three miles."

"I need some time by myself."

"You just said you were tired."

"I know but I want to think about things—like birthdays and best friends."

"You want me to drop by later?" she asked.

"No, Nate's coming over tonight."

"What about this afternoon? I can show you what I bought at the sale."

"I need to call LB. She understands."

"Only LB understands!" Emi said.

"I didn't mean it that way." I stopped. "I don't know what I meant." "Exactly."

"If you listen for a minute, I could explain."

"I don't have the time. I'll wait for the video." Emi checked the rear-view mirror. "I've got to go, Rell. The store is already open."

"Emi, I need you to be my friend," I said.

"You don't get anything, do you? I don't want to be needed!"

I took in a deep breath. "If you want me to go shopping, I will."

"Not a good idea."

"What about going out with Nate and me tonight? We

could get a pizza," I said.

"Sure, I'll ride in the back of the pickup."

No matter what I said, I made things worse.

"I'll see you," I said and I got out of the car and walked toward the sidewalk. Before I crossed the street I waited a few seconds. I was sure Emi would drive by and ask if I wanted a ride again. I waited a few more seconds before I turned around to watch her peel out of the other exit. I thought she'd circle the block then come back for me. At the traffic light I brushed imaginary hair off my cheek to check the cars behind me. No Emi.

At the intersection I squinted at oncoming cars. No Emi. Maybe she'll be in the Safeway lot, I thought. But she wasn't. So I cut through the Chevron station to the beach access.

I climbed over the chain next to the "No Trespassing" sign and headed down the path. The bougainvillea hedge had grown into a canopy of color, like a petal tunnel. The Pacific Ocean was at the other end.

The beach sand was hot and the sun was intense. I watched a wind surfer bounce through the waves. He had a lime green sail that raced across the ocean. Some kids were learning to boogie board.

I headed home, popping jellyfish under my feet as I walked. I stopped to pet a sand-covered dog and smiled at anyone I saw. Fisherman sat in chrome tube chairs guarding their lines, oil-slick tourists baked on their towels, and canoes and catamarans bobbed in the waves.

Emi and I learned how to boogie board at Kailua Beach. We built sand castles together and hunted for shells. On her thirteenth birthday Emi's parents gave her a '60s beach party at a bungalow across the canal. On her sixteenth birthday she had a spa night slumber party. We painted each other's toenails and gave each other facials.

Emi slept over at my house a lot. She thought being an only child was cool. No hand-me-down clothes, no yelling at dinner, no brothers or sisters who squealed on you. I liked it better at her house, where I could hide. As I walked I wondered what to do for Emi's birthday. I thought about buying her a gift at Island Girls and wrapping it in birthday paper then calling Sarah and Faye to have a party, but that didn't seem right. Maybe Mom and I could take her to Indigo's for a special lunch.

The sun continued to burn. After another half-hour of walking my enthusiasm waned. My purse strap dug into my shoulder and sweat trickled from under my wig. I dug through my purse to call home for a ride, but I forgot my cell phone in my room.

If I hadn't left in such a huff, I would have had it with me.

I spotted a driftwood log under an iron tree and sat in its shade for a while. *How could I have forgotten Emi's birthday?* I had photos of her all over my room.

A screeching toddler, naked except for his blue acorn cap, scampered in front of me chasing an Arctic tern.

"Charlie!" A pregnant woman lumbered to her feet.

When the bird took flight, the little boy burst into tears. Within seconds his mom scooped him up and cradled him in her chest, soothing him with kisses. "It's okay, honey." She brushed the sand from his legs and kissed him again. "Mommy's brave little hunter."

Mom to the rescue.

A gray-haired couple watched it all, too. They smiled at me. I smiled back. At the beach, life was that simple.

What's life? Life's a magazine. How much does it cost? One dollar. What's a dollar? Life. What's life? Life's a magazine.

I had another mile to walk home.

CHAPTER FIVE

When I got home Mom was standing at the kitchen sink with her hands buried in suds.

"Hi, Mom," I said.

She didn't turn around.

"I'm back."

"I didn't know you left—I didn't hear you say goodbye." She rinsed off a crystal goblet and placed it upside down on the dish rack.

"I'm sorry."

She wiped her hands on the towel. "I'm listening."

"I didn't mean to get so angry," I said, emphasizing the word "mean." "I said things that weren't true."

She tossed the towel on the counter and turned around. She leaned against the counter and crossed her arms.

"Mom, I love Ajax." That's when I noticed he wasn't in the house. "Where is Ajax?"

"He's in the garage. I just gave him a bath."

"Why?"

Did you clean him up to take him to the Humane Society?

"I bathed him because he was dirty and I'm the only one around here who does."

Score one for Mom.

"I'll give him a bath from now on, I promise."

"We'll see," was her answer.

"Mom, I'm sorry for what I said this morning."

She turned to me and rested her hands on her hips. "And for the way you said it?"

"I love Ajax," I said.

"That has nothing to do with the way you spoke to your father and me. We are not your school friends, Rell. If you want to talk to them that way, it's your business, but I am your mother and I won't tolerate it."

Trust me, my friends aren't tolerating much either.

"It won't happen again," I said. I heard Ajax scratching at the family room door. "Can I let him in?"

"He's still wet."

I knew enough not to push it. I scooted around her, gingerly, to get a drink of water. "Did Dr. Braden call back?" I held my breath waiting for her answer.

"Yes." She waited a long moment before continuing. "He said that if you were a veterinarian, there would be a health risk, but not with a household pet."

"So Ajax stays."

"Ajax stays. But I still want you to be cautious."

I tried to slither the conversation away from Ajax. I'd heard what I wanted to hear and didn't want to risk blowing it and getting her annoyed about something else. "Are you having people over to dinner?" I figured that was a safe question.

"Dad's managers are coming over to talk about the Hilo job."

"Does that mean he's not going to Guam?"

"Apparently." It was a sharp answer that didn't need any follow-up questions.

I poured myself another glass of water. "Where's Dad now?"

"He's out getting wine." She turned to me. "Rell, I could use some help getting the table set."

"Mom, I'm so tired. Can I take a nap first?"

"You had enough energy to go shopping with Emi." She just let that toad hop out of her mouth.

"Let me catch a quick nap, then I'll help," I said.

"It may be time for you to take back some of your chores, young lady."

Taking back chores was one step to normal that I didn't want to take.

"You're right," I said, then I squinted my eyes and clouded them over so I would look tired.

"Are you hungry? I could make you some lunch."

I wanted to scream out in big, bold letters, "I am not hungry!" But I said, "No, thanks" instead.

"Did you and Emi eat out?"

"We stopped at the Thai restaurant next to the dry cleaner's." It was one more lie on my path to hell. "I'll tell you all about it when I get up. They have great coconut custard." I edged myself toward the hall.

"What time do you want me to wake you up?" she asked.

"Nate's coming at five."

"I'll get you up at two so you can help me with the table."

"What about three-thirty?"

"Fine," she said. It wasn't a good "fine."

At three-thirty, Mom jolted me awake. "My God, Rell! Look at you."

I thought there was a fire.

"Look at yourself." She pointed to the dresser.

I sat up and stared at the red-lobster face in the mirror.

"You are burned to a crisp!" she said.

No denying it, I was glowing.

"You know you have to be careful about being in the sun."

Ajax came frolicking in my room.

"How could you do this, Rell?"

"I didn't plan on it, Mom."

Ajax sat at the foot of my bed, wagging his tail.

"I thought you and Emi were going shopping?"

"Plans changed," I said.

"You know you're at risk for skin cancer. How many times have I told you to wear sunscreen everyday, no matter what?"

"Mom, I always wear sunscreen."

"Obviously you didn't today."

I poked my cheek with my finger. It left a bloodless white imprint.

"Do you have any of that prescription cream for radiation burns left?"

"I think so." I jumped off the bed, headed to my bathroom before Mom went in and snooped around. Ajax followed me in, trying to stick his head in the vanity under the sink.

"Go away, boy," I said.

He thought I was playing and hunched down on his front legs.

"Not now, boy."

He barked and pivoted in a circle.

"Ajax," Mom said sharply, and he jumped on the bed right in her lap. "Get down," she yelled.

He jumped down, cut across the floor, then leapt back on my bed on to mom's lap.

Suddenly, the whole thing seemed funny to me—my

florescent face, Ajax bounding off the bed and Mom on the verge of a meltdown. It was a scene straight out of a movie.

I had a bizarre flash of Dad doing his impression of the drunken limbo dancer in the movie *Sixteen Summers*.

That was it! I finally got it! Nobody in our house laughed anymore. There were a lot of oh-my-poor-baby smiles, but there weren't any knee-slapping, belly-belching laughs.

I handed Mom the burn cream.

"Sit," she ordered me. And I sat.

I wished I could have lived in that movie. I'd be the preacher's daughter who had sex with the pool guy.

"Rell, you get me so upset."

That was the signal that I was in for one of her I'm-trying-to-be-the-best-mother-I-can-be lectures.

"Rell, do you remember Dr. Braden explaining about your risk for skin cancer?"

"Yes, Mom."

You tend to listen when doctors talk about cancer and your life.

"Rell, you are different from other girls."

No. I am not different, Mom. I am the same.

She stroked the cream over my face. "I worry when I see you do things like this."

I pictured the surfer boy in *Sixteen Summers*. His name was Rex. A wave pulled down his board shorts.

"This could have been prevented with a little common sense." She massaged the cream on my shoulders.

Rex's butt was like two plump pears.

"I know," I said.

Mom worked the cream up my neck. "Rell, I try so

hard not to be afraid for you."

Try harder, Mom.

"Last week a student of mine was diagnosed with breast cancer. She's nineteen."

I don't need to know this, Mom.

"I know she has nothing to do with you, but every time I see her, I'm reminded of cancer."

Like I'm never reminded?

I wanted to be at the limbo party in *Sixteen Summers* with some six-foot-three lifeguard pouring pina coladas down my throat. I had never been drunk in my entire life—not falling-down, puke-my-guts-out, pass-out drunk. Who was I kidding? I'd never even had a beer.

"Rell, we've been through a lot this year," Mom said. "I just don't want to do it again. I don't know if I can handle it."

She wasn't the one who the dragon was stalking. I was the one who could relapse.

"I love you, Rell. You are my Beautiful Star." She rocked me.

One more time, I felt like I had to protect her, and I resented it.

"I promise not to worry about you so much, Sweetheart," she said.

I loved my mother. "I promise to be more careful."

We were both lying.

There was a cocktail waitress in *Sixteen Summers*. She could drink a can of beer in less than fifteen seconds. I wondered if that was humanly possible. Mom was still holding me when I decided that if you held your breath and just let the beer flow down your throat, maybe it could be done.

"What time is Nate picking you up for your date?"

Mom let go of me and patted my knee.

"It's not a date," I said.

"Well, whatever it is you call it these days."

"Five."

But the cocktail waitress ends up dying in a car crash because she lets her drunken boyfriend drive her home.

"You are a beautiful young woman, Rell."

"Thanks, Mom."

"Although right now, you look more like a Waikiki tourist." She walked over to my closet and held up my blue-green jumper. "This color would make you look less red," she said.

"Good choice," I said, knowing that I was going to wear my jeans.

After Mom left I got dressed. I spun around in front of the mirror, putting my hands where my hips used to be. I had lost so much weight that I didn't have hips anymore. I didn't have a chest or a backside either. Basically, I had the figure of a ten-year-old boy. My jeans hung an inch below my belly button, just enough to show some skin but not enough to show my scar.

I wore my silver dolphin earrings and slathered sand beige heavy concealer on my face. Most of the red was invisible.

Smile, I said to myself. Let your "glowing" personality shine through.

The doorbell rang. I sprayed myself with vanilla perfume.

"Is anyone going to get the door?" Dad called out from his den.

"I've got it, Dad."

When I answered the door a dark figure with spiked black hair, wide cheekbones and duct tape over his mouth appeared. It was Nate. His eyes were shouting at me, "Go ahead, ask me what the duct tape is doing across my mouth."

I acted like there was nothing unusual. "I'm going to say good-night to my folks," I said. "I'll tell them you said 'hello.'"

When I got back I asked Nate, "Is this a new version of man talk?"

He shook his head "no."

"Is this a game?"

He nodded, "yes."

"What kind of game?"

As we walked to his truck he handed me an index card marked "Number One." Then he made a flipping motion with his hands. The back of the card read, "You can find your dreams if you follow the clues."

"Dreams? What dreams?" I asked.

He pointed again, stabbing the card.

"Okay, I'll play," I said. "Dreams? Dreams at the end of a rainbow? Are we going to Rainbow's for chicken katsu dinner?"

He shook his head "no."

"Dreams? Dreams like fortunes? We're going to Chinatown to get our fortunes told."

This time a vigorous "no."

I climbed in the truck and he closed the door behind me. As he drove away I wondered if it was legal for him to drive with duct tape across his mouth.

He pointed to card number two on the dashboard. I read it out loud. "To follow your dream you must take one step after another."

"Okay, Nate, what is this?"

He turned toward me. I thought he was smiling. His cheeks were puffed out, his eyes narrowed, and under the duct tape

I detected an upward curve of his mouth.

"One step after another," I repeated. "It's not the marathon, that's for sure." I fidgeted with the card. "Night hiking?"

He kept his eyes on the road.

"Are we going hiking?"

Another "no."

"Maybe a walk. Honolulu Time Walk? The Ghost Tour."

I was wrong again.

I thought out loud. "One step after another, but not a hike and not a walk. A street? A road? The road less traveled? The yellow brick road? The road to where? Where in the world is Carmen San Diego?" I turned to Nate. "Got it! We're flying to San Diego."

He laughed a muffled laugh and pointed to the glove box where, buried among half-eaten Lifesavers and parking stubs for Honolulu General Hospital was card number three, stuck to a crumpled-up Power Bar wrapper.

I peeled the card off and read, "Tonight you will receive a gift that was inspired by dreams."

I looked around in his truck. There was an old milk crate jammed in the cubby behind my seat, overflowing with basketball shoes, stained towels, sunscreen, dirty T-shirts and probably last week's gym clothes. "Dreams? This truck could inspire nightmares."

Nate shrugged.

We were headed into the first Pali tunnel. Between the first and second tunnel was a view of the windward side from Lanikai to the North Shore. It was my favorite view on the island.

Nate jabbed the card with his finger.

"Yes, sir." I snapped an exaggerated salute. "This is my dream that's going to come true, not yours," I said. "Fat chance of any of your dreams coming true, buster." He took his hands off the wheel, clasped them in prayer and leaned toward me in a fake plea.

"Hey! Pay attention to the road." I pointed to the car in front of us. "Fooling around on the Pali makes me very nervous."

Right outside the second tunnel was an emergency parking lot with a phone, a first-aid kit and a bench. Nate pulled over. He reached into his pocket and delivered another card: "From now on I will only go where you tell me to go. You can either continue to play or give up and never find your dream."

"I'll play," I said.

Card number five read: "The memory of its city lights brings the islander home again."

"Honolulu," I said.

By the eighth card I was standing next to the hula girl statue at the Aloha Tower Marketplace. Nate still had the duct tape over his mouth, unbothered by the stares of tourists.

One old guy in a porkpie hat and brown plaid shorts that were pulled high over his belly called over to Nate. "You look like you're in training for being married."

"Stop it, Harry." The man's wife jabbed his belly, setting off a tidal wave of fat rippling across his shirt—a rayon Aloha shirt that matched her hibiscus *mu'u mu'u*.

Nate gave Harry a thumbs up.

By time I read the last card I was in front of the cash register at the Blue Hawai'i Bookstore.

The last card said, "Hand this to the clerk and claim a gift for Estrella DeMello."

The clerk exchanged the card for what appeared to be a wrapped hardcover book.

The gift tag had Nate's handwriting. "To my Beautiful Star, From Nate."

"You know what my name means." I beamed.

Nate took a sweeping bow.

I gently pulled off the wrapping paper to uncover *The Dream of Light, A Path through the Grand Canyon*, by Makana Johns.

"I've wanted this book for so long." I threw my arms around him and kissed the duct tape across his lips. As I leafed through the book, he peeled the tape off his mouth. Silver strands of adhesive stuck to what looked like an instant rash across his face.

"You okay?" I asked.

"I think so." He patted his mouth with the back of his hand.

I stood on my tiptoes and gave him a kiss.

"Ouch."

"Ruin the moment," I said pretending to be annoyed. "Pure romance ruined by a mouth pansy."

"I'll show you 'mouth pansy.'" Nate put his arm around me, dipped me back and kissed me. "Jeez, that stings." He squeezed his eyes and pursed his lips.

"You know, for a smart guy, you get zero in common sense."

"Is that zero a mean, a median or an average?"

I wanted to give Nate a big Santa Claus hug and cover

him with hundreds of kisses. I hugged him again and told him, "This is the best gift I ever got."

He beamed with "man pride."

"Are you ready for what's next?" he said.

"There's more?"

"You bet."

The more was more fries, more ketchup and more beef in your burger. We ate at Bruddah's Grill at the end of the Aloha Tower pier at a table overlooking the harbor. The SS *Independence* cruise ship was berthed next to us. It was all lit up like a birthday cake with strung white lights for candles and red and blue streamers for frosting. Halfway through our meal I felt a low-pitched rumble—the pier vibrated and the ship got underway. Her horn blasted, little girls in ti-leaf skirts danced hula on the dock, and right on cue, a helicopter showered the ship with plumeria blossoms. It was just like the movies. I reached over for Nate's hand and braided my fingers into his.

He handed me a napkin with his other hand. "You want to wipe the ketchup off your hands first?"

I crumpled the napkin and threw it at him. "Right after you quit the red-lipped reindeer routine."

"Wound me," he said, grasping his heart.

"I already did."

Our waitress refilled our drinks then rested the pitcher of water on her hip. "Are you on vacation?" she asked.

"Yes. We're from San Francisco," Nate answered.

"You may want to stick around." She lifted her pitcher in the direction of Diamond Head. "The Hilton puts on a fireworks show in fifteen minutes."

"Thanks, we will," I said.

The night was perfect. I wanted to turn it into a nine by twelve glossy photo, framed in gold and forever perfect. I twirled a vandah orchid from my plate between my fingers. "Thanks. It was perfect—the game, the ship, the book. It means so much to me." Nate reached for my hand. "I hope you get to go on your trip."

"No hoping about it. We're going just as soon as we figure out how to pay for it."

Nate looked at his watch. "What about Make A Wish Foundation? I bet they'd pay for it."

"I've had enough of being a cancer kid," I said. "Even if my best friend doesn't think so," I muttered under my breath. "I turn sixteen this summer, then I can get a job at The Great Outdoors. They give their employees a thirty percent discount, so I can buy all the stuff for LB and me."

"You're serious about this trip."

"You bet. LB found a tour company that might hire us to take pictures."

"Do you think she'll be able to handle the hiking?" Nate checked his watch again.

"She had some pain in her joints last week and she's tired, but that's normal." It wasn't exactly a lie.

"You never told me what the LB stands for." Nate motioned over the waitress.

I hunched over a bit. "Lightbulb Head. I know it sounds awful, but it isn't really. Her real name is Elizabeth. Tess started to call her Lightbulb Head because when her hair fell out her head almost glowed. Then it got shortened to Light Bulb, then to LB, and LB stuck."

He looked at his watch again. "Rell, why don't you order

dessert for us? I've got to go back and feed the parking meter. Give me five minutes," he said as he stood up.

"We can just stop at Bubbies for ice cream," I said. I grabbed my purse and the book.

"You don't mind missing the fireworks?" he asked.

"We can make some of our own." I winked.

What a jerky thing to say. .

We never stopped at Bubbies that night. We drove the long way home, through Sandy Beach and Waimanalo. Soft rock played on the radio and Nate held my hand as he drove.

"You want to stop at the beach?" I asked.

"Sure." He grinned.

I felt like an evil temptress.

Nate pulled in the same parking spot. We walked down the same beach path, but this time our arms rested on each other's waists. This time he carried a straw mat rolled under his arm, this time the waves were stronger, the surf louder, the tide higher, the kisses more frenzied. It was like Nate lost control and that perfect night was gone, taken over by a little boy's hunger.

"Stop." I pushed him away.

He looked at me like he didn't know why I did it.

"I thought your mouth was hurting," I said.

"Not anymore." He leaned his head on my shoulder. I scooted back on the mat and drew my knees up to my chest. "Lots of stars," I said, staring up at the sky.

Nate edged over to me, put his arm around my waist and nuzzled the back of my neck with his face. I felt like he was Ajax, digging his snout into my neck for a biscuit that was there a week before.

"Looks like the tide's coming in," I said.

"Uh-huh." Nate kissed behind my ears.

I took in a deep breath. "The moon's full."

He didn't stop.

If he pushes his head any higher up my ear, he's going to knock off my wig. I had visions of it floating out to sea like a soggy mongoose sprawled on a wave.

"Nate, don't." I pushed him away.

"What's wrong?"

Lots of things. I figured he'd had sex before and I knew that I didn't.

I could feel him working his kisses up my neck. All I could think of was my wig. I was sure it was tilted on my head like a French sailor in a drug-bust movie. I tugged at it, hoping he would figure out to leave it alone. But he put his arm around me again and coaxed my head on his shoulder. He was touching my wig.

"My wig!" I pulled away.

"I'm sorry."

I was so embarrassed I wanted to follow a sand crab down a hole.

"I didn't mean it," Nate said.

"It's okay." I drew my knees tight to my chest and cradled them with my arms. I rested my chin on my knees. For a few minutes we didn't talk.

"What's your hair look like under there?" he asked.

I wanted to say "like a chemo patient's out of treatment," but only LB would get that joke. I looked at his face, his almond eyes edged with short stubby lashes. "Like a newborn Chinese baby's."

He laughed. "So it sticks out everywhere?"

"And it's short," I said.

"It can't be shorter than Tia Kiakona's," he said.

"Tia's hair is styled. Mine is growing in."

"Let me see."

"No."

"You've got to take it off sometime. Besides, who's out here to see?"

You.

He rubbed my back. "It's okay, Rell."

"It's stubby," I said.

"It's probably not as bad as you think."

"And parts of it look like duck down. You know, fuzzy."

"I heard fuzzy is in these days."

I slipped my hands under the elastic edging.

What if he laughs at me?

"You want some help?" He leaned forward.

"No!" I coiled.

"Sorry."

Now I hurt his feelings.

I lifted the wig straight up, the whole time thinking what a dumb thing it was to do. "Well?" I faced him.

He was supposed to say, "It looks great," or smile or clap or do something positively wonderful. But all he did was stare.

"Well?" I repeated.

"Give me a minute," he said.

Give you a minute. I just took off my wig and you say, "Give me a minute."

I grabbed for my wig.

Nate put his hand over mine. "It doesn't look bad."

Doesn't look bad? How not bad? Like a worn out tennis ball not bad?

"I'm going to put it back on."

He tightened his grip on my arm. "It's not bad, honest."

Wow! I can't handle all the compliments!

"You look fine, Rell." Nate cradled my chin in his hands. "Look at me, Rell," he whispered.

I wouldn't look up.

He kissed me and I started to cry.

"It's okay, Rell." He kissed the top of my head—my patchy, limp hair, scaly head.

"How can you even look at me?"

"You're beautiful, Rell." He kissed me again, this time more intensely, and leaned me back on the mat. I jumped back up.

"What did I do now?" he said.

"Stop it." This was the other half of the game, I thought. Get her to take off her wig, humiliate her, and then get her to have sex. "You're a real asshole," I said.

"I'm an asshole?" He jabbed his finger into his chest. "Forty bucks for a book. I waste my whole day making stupid index cards and I'm an asshole."

He had a point.

"You don't understand," I said.

"I'm trying to," he said.

"You have no idea."

He shook his head. "You're right. I have no idea. You said you had the best night ever, the best present ever, and I'm an asshole."

I put my hand in his and said, "Sometimes I get scared."

"Welcome to the world, Rell. We're all scared of something."

"I was afraid of taking off my wig," I said.

"And you did it and it's over."

Another Nathan Lee mathematical formula: fear of taking off a wig minus taking off a wig equals no fear.

"I want to be regular again," I said.

"Constipation got you down?"

"Forget it." I pulled back my hand.

"I'm not a mind reader, Rell."

"All right, I'll try to explain." I sat cross-legged facing him. "There was a first grader who left Stanhope about three months before I did. She finished her treatment and she was healthy and she went back to school." I turned to Nate. "You sure you want to hear this?"

"I'm sure." But I could hear annoyance in his voice.

"Then one day she told her teacher that her father was beating her up just so she could get attention. It was a lie." I looked over at him. "She was afraid of being a regular kid."

"That doesn't make any sense."

"I told you that you wouldn't understand."

"Rell, this girl was in first grade. You're fifteen."

"It doesn't matter," I said. "She couldn't move past her cancer. It's not that easy."

"I know," he said.

You don't know.

"Are you ever afraid?" I asked him.

"Sometimes," he said.

"Of what?"

"When I was at St. Luke's, Samuel Larsen came to talk to us."

"The movie director?"

"Yeah."

I felt a chill. A shiver shuddered down my back. I

huddled closer to Nate to get warm, and then I realized that for the first time in months there was a breeze on my head.

"Larsen said great movies always have great characters."

"There's big news," I said.

"He said the key to creating great characters is to remember that all people are afraid and all people are lonely."

I lifted my head.

"He said it's the way people deal with their fear that makes them who they are."

"And?" I asked.

"There's the public way—the way we show everyone else, or how we pretend to be brave, then there are the private times, when we're alone and we have to face fear head-on."

"This coming from a guy who makes movies about car chases?" I said.

"But he made sense, Rell." He straightened his back and waved his hands in the air as he explained. "Don't you get it? Some people pretend to be brave by becoming bullies, or athletes, or driving fast cars. Some people write poetry, but in some way, we're all trying to drive away the fear."

"So all I need to do is to drive a fast car and my cancer won't come back?"

"All you have to do is figure out what you're afraid of and deal with it."

"Is that all, oh great Chinese philosopher?" I mocked.

"Do you think your cancer will come back?"

You're not supposed to ask questions like that. It's not polite.

"My doctor said it's normal to be afraid of relapse," I answered.

"Nice lateral pass, Rell," Nate said. "Let's try it again.

Does your doctor think that your cancer will come back?"

"They don't talk like that. They talk about survival rates after five years. It's all numbers to them."

"Are yours good?"

Nate Lee wanted another mathematical formula.

"My numbers are good. The event-free survival rate after five years is 84 percent."

"Then your odds are good."

"Right," I said.

It was the other 16 percent I was worried about.

"What about you? You didn't answer me. What are you afraid of?"

"That I'll waste one minute of my life."

Emi was right. Nate was too intense.

That night Nate and I didn't fall into passionate lovemaking, but in some ways we moved closer. Trust wasn't the right word, comfortable wasn't it either. Maybe we opened up parts of us that were secret before.

We strolled back to the truck hand-in-hand and before he opened the door, he kissed my forehead.

On the ride home my wig was in my lap. I twirled strands of it between my fingers. Without my wig I felt lighter, freer, like I took off a mask, but I missed the mask— it made me feel safe.

Nate and I were singing along with the radio when the pain hit—a sharp stab at the base of my skull. I got them at Stanhope—headaches that sliced through me like a heated razor. Within seconds the pain was in the back of my eyes— white-hot pain. My blood surged. I felt nauseous. I breathed shallowly, trying to keep the pain from getting worse.

"Why'd you stop singing?" Nate looked over.

I pressed my hands to my temples. My eyes were closed.

"You okay, Rell?"

"Bad headache." I could hardly talk.

"Do you have medicine with you?"

"No."

"Should I take you to the hospital?"

"No. Just home." Each word set off a throbbing reaction.

"Should I pull over?"

"Home."

I made it home. Nate walked me to the door. Dad's managers were still in the dining room. I went to my room, straight for the medicine cabinet and gulped down some Tylenol with codeine.

It's an ordinary headache, I told myself. *The headache bone is not connected to the cancer bone.* I went to bed and lay as still as I could. *Headaches are not a symptom of cancer. Repeat, one hundred times.*

CHAPTER SIX

The next morning I felt fine. Mom nudged me awake. "LB's on the phone," she said.

"Tell her I'll call her back." I was still asleep.

"She's crying," Mom said.

I rolled over and reached for my phone. "Hey, LB what's up?" I tried to sound upbeat.

"I know it's early there, Rell, but I have to talk."

"Never too early for you."

"I'm scared, Rell." I could hear her crying.

"What's the matter?"

"I heard the nurses talking about a bone marrow test for me on Tuesday. I'm not scheduled for one until next month."

"Maybe it's a scheduling error. You know how things get mixed up."

"I called the lab. It's not a mistake."

I said, "There could be lots of reasons for this," although none of them were good.

"This is serious, Rell."

I asked the usual litany of questions. "How's your weight?"

"I lost three pounds last week, but I wasn't eating much."

"What about your blood tests?"

"Not good. Dr. Lynch ran them again."

"Has he stopped your treatments?"

"Yes." She paused. "And I have a fever of 101 degrees."

We both knew she was in trouble, not seriously, but in

trouble. LB had leukemia when she was two, but this time her cancer was refractory—it wouldn't respond to treatment. When I first got to Stanhope she was on her last three months of standard treatment. When that failed, she had a bone marrow transplant, and when that failed she started an experimental trial.

"Dr. Lynch brought in another doctor to see me. He's from Seattle."

"Fred Hutch?"

"Uh-huh."

Part of having cancer was to have a vocabulary that included too many medical terms and being able to rank oncology centers according to their specialty. Fred Hutchinson was strong in leukemia research.

"LB."

She was sobbing.

"LB."

If I were with her, I knew I could get her to laugh. I could pop in a silly video on the TV or go into my court-jester routine. Or I could sit next to her bed and we could talk, and if she didn't want to talk I could just sit and hold her hand. "What did the doc from Fred Hutch say?" I asked.

"The usual 'How are you, young lady' kind of stuff." I could hear her sniffling. "He read over my chart for a long time then I saw him and Dr. Lynch at the nurses' station." She stopped to catch her breath. "Then Dr. Braden was paged and the three of them were there together."

"Okay, LB, let's think about what's happening." I wanted to be logical. "It might not be as bad as you think."

Then, with a frightening calm she said, "Rell, I'm going

to die."

"Don't say that." I felt useless.

"Last night was the first time I really believed it. I always knew it could happen, but I never believed it before."

"Stop it, LB. We've got to think! Did you ask Dr. Lynch why he stopped treatment?"

"I didn't have to ask, Rell. I know why."

"You don't know why. You don't have any facts."

"Rell, they called my parents to come up this weekend."

"That makes sense. The guy from Fred Hutch probably wants to talk to them about a new treatment."

"They think I'm going to die."

I knew she could be right, but maybe the Fred Hutch guy just wanted to talk to them about a new treatment. Maybe the bone marrow test was to find out if she was a good candidate. There were a lot of maybes. But when I tried to say that, all that came out was, "LB, if you want me to be there, I'll fly out tomorrow."

She laughed. "Superwoman Rell flies across the ocean on her magic carpet."

"The flying carpet's at the cleaner's," I said.

Then it was quiet.

"You okay?" I asked.

Nothing.

"LB?"

"I've got to go, Rell."

"I love you, LB."

"Right back at you, Roomie." And she hung up.

I sat on my bed cradling the phone. It was a little after ten o'clock in the morning in San Francisco. At Stanhope the morning teaching rounds were starting. By eleven-thirty the lunch carts would line the hall. Then the nurses would come in to check our vital signs. Later the docs would visit their patients. Dinner came next, then the evening shift came on and more vital signs were taken. Every day was the same.

The night cleaning lady came in about seven o'clock. She wore white running shoes and orange scrubs. Her name was Mrs. Bajak. She was from Poland.

The first thing she did when she came in was say, "Just for you, Moon Beam," and she'd put some hard candy on my bed stand. Mrs. Bajak had a strong accent and her stories were always the same—about her daughter who was an honor student at Oakland High.

I felt safe in the hospital. There were always nurses around who asked if I had a good night and the doctors were only a page away, and if I needed to talk, there were plenty of kids like me who understood.

When I was at Stanhope I couldn't wait to be home. But now that I was home, there were times I wanted to back in the hospital. That's something Emi could never understand. I rolled over and tried to get back to sleep. But all I could do was lie there. I turned over. I punched my pillow and punched it again. Then I let the tears flow.

Later that day I called Emi. I dialed her number but after two rings I hung up.

What if she doesn't want to talk to me?

When I dialed again Kalani answered. He said he thought Emi was in the garage. But when he got back he said, "Rell, I can't find her. My dad said she went out with her friends. Are you supposed to meet her somewhere?"

"Yeah," I lied. I was sure Emi was standing right next to him, mouthing "Tell her I'm not here."

Emi and I never had a fight that lasted overnight. I sat in my room and worked on my English homework: eight lines of non-rhyming poetry. Nothing was working. Every poem I wrote was about LB and every one was bad.

So, I called Sarah and asked her to go to the movies. *The Tin Box* was playing at the mall.

"Sure," she said. With Sarah things were so easy.

I got dressed, put on my makeup and my Hat-Hair wig and gave myself a final check in the mirror. Then I took off the Hat-Hair. "No wig," I said. "No more." And I took it off. Then I put it back on, and then I took it off again.

When it was time to go Mom picked up her purse and said, "Ready." She didn't flinch. She asked me what movie we were going to see and what time to pick me up. I could tell she was trying not to look at my head.

In the car I flipped through the stations. Halfway to the mall I said, "I've decided to go 'topless.'"

"I noticed," Mom said.

"And I noticed you didn't say anything."

"Not that I didn't want to." Mom turned to me.

"Don't ruin it, Mom. You're doing so well." I smiled.

When she dropped me off I gave her an especially big hug, thankful that she was beginning to let go, then I darted in the mall. The doors swung open like a curtain pulling back on a daytime drama. I made eye contact with two ladies walking out of Banana Republic. They halted their conversation. One of them smiled at me, that Oh-my-God-she-has-no-hair-she-must-have-cancer kind of smile.

I smiled back.

The clerk at the garden kiosk stopped watering her plants. I wanted to go up to her and ask if she's never seen a bald girl before, but I ran down to the movie theater instead.

A moving target is harder to see.

Sarah was waiting for me in front of Godiva's. "Great look!" She spun me around twice and rubbed my scalp. "Great shaped head. Not a flat spot anywhere."

"Thanks. I think."

A couple of guys passed us. They elbowed each other and turned back, snickering. I felt embarrassed for Sarah, like some of my cancer spilled over on her.

"What about a tattoo on the back of your head?" Sarah asked.

"Only you could pull that off," I said.

Sarah was dressed in a mauve gauze skirt and a smocked midriff top. Her new fad was wearing antique-bell ankle bands that tinkled when she walked.

"Another bracelet?" It was a leather band with round brass bells.

"It's Egyptian," she answered. "I'm thinking of taking Middle Eastern dance—you know, with veils," she said.

"You mean belly dancing?"

"It's more complicated than that."

I raised my eyebrows.

"It's cultural," she said.

Sarah was the smartest person I knew. She had a perfect GPA, took Advanced Placement Physics and French, but you'd never know it. She treated the world like it was her fan club and thought everyone loved her. Why not? It's the way she felt about the world.

"I'm even wearing Egyptian musk." She took a vial out of her purse and put it under my nose then dabbed some on a ten-dollar bill before she gave it to the ticket seller.

"It'll make the cash drawer smell good," she said.

We sat halfway up the theatre in the absolute middle. My seat was under a draft aimed directly at my head. I twisted away from the chilled air. I tugged my T-shirt over my chin and curled down in the seat. Every time I heard someone cough I worried about catching whatever the air was spreading.

After the show Sarah asked me if I liked the movie.

"It was pretty good," I said.

I pointed to Tropical Freeze ice cream parlor and Sarah answered with a nod. "So that was you having a good time?" she asked.

"Uh-huh."

"You jiggled your foot during the whole movie."

"It's a nervous habit," I said.

"You sat there with your hands tucked under your armpits."

"I was cold."

"You should have said something. We could have moved."

If I said something I wouldn't have been normal.

Tropical Freeze had a movie review board. Instead of stars, or thumbs up, customers posted ice cream magnets next to the title of the movie.

I gave *The Tin Box* a review of two ice creams cones. Sarah gave it four.

When I went to order my ice cream the counter guy gave me wink and said, "Nice hair." If his head wasn't shaved and his nails weren't painted black, I would have taken the compliment seriously.

Sarah and I ate at the counter next to the window.

"What were the kids like when you were in the hospital?" Sarah asked.

"Basic kids," I said digging into my Lahaina Sundae.

"Did the little kids know they were dying?" She asked it in a matter-of-fact way while she piled her M&M toppings on the side.

She noticed me watching her make the pile. "I like to eat them last," she said. "Did the kids know they could die?" she repeated.

"Some," I answered. "Some were too young to understand."

"Sad." When she crossed her legs, the bells tinkled. "Did you have any gene therapy?" she asked.

"How do you know about gene therapy?" I couldn't believe someone who didn't have cancer even heard of that kind of stuff.

"Remember me? Sarah Reynolds, brain geek. When you got sick, I looked up Hodgkin's disease on the Internet." She licked her spoon. "I read everything there was at the National Institute of Health."

"You may know more than I do," I said.

"I said that I read it, that doesn't mean I understood it."

I wondered if she read anything about LB's leukemia. "Did you read anything about leukemia?" I asked.

"Yeah," she said. "Most of the lymphoma stuff was lumped in with leukemia."

"Did you ever hear of ANL?"

Sarah could change from being absent-minded to being sharply focused, as casually as she piled the M&Ms on the side of her plate. She stared blankly out the window. Her eyes seemed to be scanning information stored in her brain. "Did you know they were working on a vaccine against Hodgkin's disease?"

"Uh-huh," I said. "But what about ANL?"

"No, I don't remember anything." She leaned over and banged on the window.

Faye, Sharlene and Emi were walking by. My best friend, Emi, was walking by with Sharlene and Faye.

Sarah motioned them in.

"Rell, you look fantastic." Faye feathered the fuzz on my head with her fingers.

"It's a lot longer than I thought it was," Sharlene said.

"Look." I felt Faye picking my hair straight up. "Rell, you should spike it." She turned to Sharlene. "It would be wild in purple."

"My parents would love it," I said.

I spotted Emi at the door. She didn't come in.

"Henna highlights would work," Sharlene said.

Emi and I looked at each other then she walked away.

Faye said, "We're going to see *The Tin Box*."

"Sarah and I just saw it." I wanted to make sure that it got back to Emi that I wasn't sitting home waiting for her to call me back.

"What did you think?" Sharlene asked.

Sarah gave it a thumbs up, I gave it a thumbs down. But I wasn't looking at Sharlene; I was distracted watching Emi. She was standing in front of a shoe store with her back to me. She can't face me, I thought. Or, maybe she's still mad. I played out both in my head.

That night when I got home I wrote Emi a three-page

letter. Some of the ink floated in puddles of tears. After I read the letter I ripped it up into hundreds of ragged pieces and tossed them in the trash. Then I started a second letter that I never finished.

I'll see her tomorrow at school, I thought. I'll talk to her there.

Homework, I ordered myself. It was Sunday night and I still had to write my poem for English.

I stared at the computer screen and waited for inspiration. It didn't come. I pressed out the photo of Tess with my hand. "Got any ideas, Tess? Anything. It doesn't have to be serious." I felt like one of the old church ladies kneeling in front of a statue waiting for it to come alive. "Anything, Tess. Anything at all." Then I remembered a poem Tess wrote about cancer—that it grew inside of her like a dark light.

For me, cancer was different.

I Am A Weed
by Estrella DeMello

*I was damaged and scarred
and still I flourished
Like a weed breaking through the sidewalk
not knowing I was strong.
I raised my flower face to the sun,
I grew a thick stem and thorns so sharp
that no one could touch me.
I grew on my own.*

It was Monday morning. To wig or not to wig, that was the question. Whether it was better to risk the smirks of fools or hide under my wig forever.

I opted for no wig. But my strategy called for distraction. I layered my five eyelashes with "volumizing" mascara and stuffed my bra with gym socks. I yanked out the socks.

During breakfast I told Mom, "I'm thinking of going to school like this." I pointed to my head. "What do you think?"

"What do you think?" She passed the question right back at me.

"I'm not sure."

"You could bring your wig with you, just in case you change your mind," Mom said.

"I don't think so." But I already had stuffed it in my purse.

"How did you feel without it at the mall?"

"A guy at Tropical Freeze said my hair was nice." I didn't bother to mention his shaved head and black fingernails.

I got into the car and strapped myself in like I was an astronaut being launched to the moon.

"Are you sure you don't want to bring your wig with you?" Mom asked.

"I'm sure."

Why did she force me to lie?

When Mom pulled up to school she reached for my hand. "You keep your chin up, your shoulders back and walk in there like you own the place." It was like she was ordering me into battle. "You are beautiful, Rell. Don't forget that." She was smiling with everything but her eyes.

"Thanks, Mom." I felt like Joan of Arc. And as corny as her speech sounded, I wore Mom's words like armor. But when I got to the door, the armor melted. I pictured kids throwing their hands over their eyes, running for cover, doors slamming and the PA screeching, "Rell DeMello took off her wig."

I wanted to run away, but I froze with my hand on the door. I wanted to disappear, forever in limbo. But you had to die to get to limbo and death wasn't an option—not on the steps of Kailua High on a Monday morning with the whole school watching.

"This is it," I said to myself. "Put one foot in front of the other." I clasped my books to my chest and inhaled. "When you walk, keep your chin parallel to the floor. Expand the space between your waist and the bottom of your ribs. Walk from your thighs, not your knees." I read that in *Seventeen* magazine.

I walked in. The walls didn't crumble. There was no lightning, no floods, no floors opened up and swallowed me whole.

Boys straight ahead.

They walked by. They didn't stare. No backward glances. No lingering snickers. They didn't care.

But girls care, I thought. They'll keep me "the girl with cancer" forever. They'll make us a couple. Cancer, King of the Prom and his Homecoming Queen, Estrella DeMello.

Jennifer Oshima was heading straight for me. "Hi Rell. Great hair," she said.

Jennifer wasn't a fair test. She was a born-again Christian and a cheerleader.

"How very wow!" from Deborah Misaki. She didn't count either. Deborah was always drugged.

I walked down the hall smiling, with my head up,

hearing my mother's words. It worked until I got to my locker and Emi turned the corner. She looked at my head. She didn't say anything, and I couldn't read her expression. "You want to talk?" I asked.

She opened her locker, using the door as a shield between us.

I stepped to the other side. "Emi." I tried to get her to look at me. "Emi, please."

"I have nothing to say." She shifted books around in her locker.

"I'm sorry," I said. It seemed like I was apologizing to everyone.

A few kids passed us, jostling each other. The morning locker jam was at its peak. Paul Cruz called out, "Looking sexy, Rell."

Emi rolled her eyes.

"Was that my fault, too?" I said. "Did I tell Paul to say that?"

Emi closed her locker door, not slamming it, but lifting the handle in a controlled, calculated move. "Do you even know what you're sorry for, Rell?"

"I was selfish," I said. "But I needed to be."

"You got pretty good at it," Emi said.

"Emi, when you're sick, really sick, all you can think about is yourself."

She didn't say anything. Jack Flynn came over and handed Emi a biology lab workbook. He looked at me and said, "Good for you, Rell. That takes guts."

When he left she said, "One more time, Rell, The Heroic Cancer Survivor."

"Emi, I took the wig off because of you. It's not my

fault I'm getting attention."

"You love it."

"Emi, when you're in the hospital everybody is watches you all the time, every little thing you do—it's hard to explain. Everything is about you. Everybody is about you."

"Well, I'm not about you," Emi said.

"I'm trying to explain."

"You're not doing a good job."

I was beginning to wonder if it was worth it. "Emi."

"Don't say another word." Emi's back stiffened.

"Emi, listen."

"Don't talk!" she said. "Wanda's right behind you."

"Re-el." Her voice sounded like a cat in heat. "Well, look at you." She ran her hand over my scalp. She touched my head.

My shoulders tensed, my face flushed. I wanted to pounce on her, rip out her hair and tear out her tongue. *I am not public property. You cannot go around touching other people's heads!*

"You really are a courageous soul," she was almost purring.

I was seething.

Emi grabbed my arm. "Rell, we have to go. Come on, we're late."

I scrambled for my books.

"What's the rush?" Wanda asked.

"We're meeting with Mr. Owens. He's starting a peer sensitivity group." Emi dragged me down the hall. "We're supposed to be there already."

"What's the group about?" Wanda asked.

"How not to be an asshole," Emi answered.

I half-waved. "Bye, Wanda."

The two of us sprinted down the hall and around the corner. Then we collapsed against the wall. "Safe," Emi said.

"Until next time," I said.

"How'd you like the sensitivity group idea?" Emi smiled.

"Brilliant."

Emi crossed her eyes and stuck out her tongue. "Wanda Yamanaka, poster child for the sensitivity impaired."

The first-period bell rang. Emi and I looked at each other. "Emi, I am sorry about your birthday. I promise next year you'll have the best birthday party in the whole world. Compliments of yours truly."

"I don't want a party, Rell. I just want us not to fight."

I stood up, swung my backpack over my shoulder and reached up to adjust my wig. But the wig wasn't there.

Emi stroked the top of my head with her hand. "Jack Flynn is right. You do have guts coming to school like this."

"A friend of mine told me I should quit wearing my wig like it was some kind of merit badge."

"Your friend should think before she says things."

"I think she was right," I said, "but just in case." I opened my purse and showed her my Hat-Hair wig. "I've got the situation covered."

Emi leaned over and gave me a hug. The corner of her books hit two inches away from my scar. "Do you remember the last time we fought like that?" she asked.

I shook my head.

"It was when we were thirteen and you told Sarah that I was afraid I was really a boy because I didn't get my period yet."

I covered my face with my hands. "Did I do that?"

"It was a low blow. But Sarah was cool with it," Emi said.

"Sarah is very cool," I said. "And so are Faye and Sharlene."

And with that we each forgave the other for going to the mall with other people. As we walked to my class I asked her, "What did you think of The Tin Box?"

She gave it a thumbs down.

"Me too," I said.

When we got to the door of my English class, I froze. "Emi, I can't do this. I've got to put the wig on."

"Paul Cruz just told you looked sexy."

"Paul thinks urinals are sexy."

"Just walk in."

"I can't."

"Fine, then put the wig on," Emi said. "I'll get Wanda to help you. It'll make a great story for the school paper." Emi waved her hand through the air, reading an imaginary headline. "The girl who wasn't courageous enough to give up her wig."

A surge of anti-Wanda shot through me. "You know just what buttons to push, don't you?"

"That's what friends are for." She grinned.

"I wish you could come in with me."

"Rell, I'm late for biology." She pushed me in the door.

My grandstand-PA-blaring-naked-head entrance was a nonevent. I got a few smiles, a few blank stares, nothing out of the ordinary.

Halfway through class I realized I hadn't seen Nate, and on Sunday night he hadn't called. I checked my pager. No pages. Between English and History class Nate still wasn't around.

Maybe he's sick, I thought to myself. At the beginning of

History I wondered what could be wrong with him. By the end of class I was sure that we had broken up.

It was the wig. I shouldn't have taken it off. It was too much for him. Or maybe it was because we didn't have sex.

Walking in the cafeteria I could hear everyone whisper, "Nate Lee dumped Rell DeMello."

"I think we broke up," I told Emi. "We had a fight Saturday night. Well, not a fight, but, I don't know."

"What did you fight about?"

I didn't answer her. Instead I said, "He didn't call me last night. He always calls on Sunday night."

"Always?" Emi asked.

"Most of the time."

"Maybe it's for the best," Emi said.

I ignored the remark. "Maybe we didn't break up. Maybe his truck broke down on the road somewhere and that's why he's not at school today. Last weekend it took three tries before it would start. Or maybe his relatives came to visit from California."

"Or maybe his mother has cancer." As soon as she said it, she stiffened. "Oh, Rell. I am so sorry."

"It's okay," I said.

"That was an awful thing to say."

"It would have been hilarious at Stanhope," I said.

"Nate could be sick." Emi said it like it was an apology for her cancer remark.

"I don't think he'd just dump me like that. He's too nice a guy."

"Not everybody thinks so," she said.

"What do you mean?"

The fifth-period bell rang. Neither of us got up.

"Emi, what do you know about Nate?"

"Nothing."

"You're a lousy liar."

"It's not me, it's Kalani." She pursed her lips. "He said Nate has a bad temper."

"How?"

"I guess Nate beat up one of his friends for no reason. They were playing basketball and this guy blocked Nate's shot and he cold-cocked him."

"Nate Lee, math geek, one step removed from the kickboxing ring?"

"He said Nate kept coming back every night, just picking fights with guys on the court."

"And Kalani is sure it was Nate?"

"You know my brother, he has to pretend that he knows everything about everybody," she said.

"So why tell me now?" I asked.

"Just in case."

"Emi, can you picture Nate fighting?"

"No."

When I got home that afternoon there were no phone messages from Nate. No bouquet of flowers, no skywriting, no fireworks, no truckloads of chocolate in gold-foil cartons. I sat cross-legged on my bed with a bowl of Rocky Road ice cream on my lap, propped my history book against my pillow and stared at the phone. I read two paragraphs and I stared at the phone. I turned three pages and stared at the phone, then I went back to the beginning of the chapter because I didn't remember a word.

At four-thirty, Nate called. "Where were you today?" I asked.

"Whoa! Can we start out with a 'hello?'"

"I was worried about you," I said

"I have a mother for that, thank you."

"I went into school bald today."

"You're not bald, Rell."

"Where were you?"

"I had some family business to take care of," he said.

"That's it?"

"Relax, Rell. I had stuff to get done for my mom, so I figured while I was at it, I could get my truck inspected."

"I needed to talk to you."

Why did I say needed?

"So talk."

"Nevermind."

The next eternal minute we said nothing.

"Rell, I can't read your mind."

"Did you ever play basketball in Lanikai?"

"You needed to know if I play basketball in Lanikai?"

"No, I was just wondering if you did. Emi's brother said he knew you."

"I used to. Now I play at the courts behind the police station."

The police station? "Why there?"

"You don't have to pay for the lights at night."

"Okay," I said.

"Well, I'm glad I have your approval." His voice was cutting.

"I was wondering why you weren't in school, but you just told me."

Stop blubbering, I told myself. Talk about normal stuff. "Cyril had a minor seizure because I got to class late," I said. "There's not too much homework. What time are you coming over?"

"Can you get through your homework alone?"

"Why?"

"My parents don't ask this many questions, Rell."

"Sorry."

"I'm going to Paul's house. He needs help with his brother's twenty-first birthday party."

"I didn't think you hung out with Paul."

"Rell, I will see you tomorrow."

"Wait," I said.

"What?"

"Have fun."

"I will." He hung up.

I sounded desperate, distressed, anxious, hopeless, stupid and whiney. Worst of all I sounded whiney.

I got another bowl of ice cream and emailed LB. As soon as I signed on she wrote, "I wish you were here."

"Me, too," I answered.

"You were right about the Fred Hutch doc. He wants me to try a new treatment."

"At Stanhope or in Seattle?"

"Seattle."

"When do you leave?"

"Right after they get this infection under control. I may

have pneumonia."

"How are you otherwise?"

"I've been having nosebleeds a lot and I'm getting platelets."

Nick had nosebleeds right before he died. The last time I saw him was my last day at Stanhope. I left a lipstick kiss on the top of his head, spreading a creamy red smudge on his forehead. "To keep you loved by Rell," I told him. He died two weeks later.

"Rell, if things don't go well, will you come to visit me?" LB asked.

"Just say the word, Roomie."

The next night her email was worse. Her parents had arrived that morning and that afternoon she had a seizure. The doctors said it was a reaction to her drugs and "not that uncommon." I shut down the computer and prayed, not to some white-bearded God, but to kids who died from cancer. "Please, don't let LB die." I knew they wouldn't let me down.

CHAPTER SEVEN

A few days later LB was doing better, and so were Nate and I. But sometimes, when Nate and I were studying or we were at the movies, I had a flash of LB—dying.

Thoughts of LB crept into my days, and in Spanish class one day I had a vision of being at her funeral. I almost called Dr. Maitlin, but I didn't.

When I showed up for my next appointment with Dr. Maitlin, the first thing she said when she saw me was, "Wow! No wig."

I brushed the top of my head with my hand. "Yeah," I said.

"Your hair looks like it has a curl to it," she said.

On the way into her office I checked myself out in the two-way mirror. "Maybe a little more curl than before."

Dr. Maitlin settled into her leather chair.

"How did it go at school without your wig?" she asked.

"A couple of kids stared," I said.

"Anything else?"

"When I was in the girls' room, I watched a girl walking behind me sneak a look at me in the mirror. But most kids were okay. So, I guess I'm a normal kid again, except for LB." I wanted to get to the point.

"What's happening with her?" Dr. Maitlin asked.

"Lots of stuff." My tears were already fighting to get out. "LB is dying," I said.

Dr. Maitlin leaned forward. "Let's talk about that, Rell."

I nodded.

"How do you feel?"

"Sad."

"What else?"

"A little scared."

"In what way?"

"I don't know." I shrugged.

"Try to explain it to me."

"It's like I'm Cinderella and it's right before midnight." I looked up at her. "Do you know what I mean?"

"I think so."

"Do you think I'm crazy?"

"No." She smiled. "Not at all." She leaned even more forward, resting her elbows on her knees.

I kept my head down. On the way over on the bus, I ate an orange. My nails still had some of the white pith under them. It looked like I had a French manicure.

"Rell, what would happen if the clock did strike midnight?"

"I'll die."

She didn't say anything right away, then, in a soft voice she said, "It's natural for you to be afraid, Rell. Your best friend is dying from the same disease that you had."

"No," I almost shouted. "She has leukemia."

"But you both had cancer," she said.

Mine was different. I had Hodgkin's disease. It's a good cancer.

"Rell, for awhile, anyone's illness, even a movie star's or someone very old, may trigger a fear of death. With LB, she's very close to you and it's much harder."

I didn't say anything.

"And, sometimes when someone relapses or doesn't respond to treatment, we experience a feeling of relief that it was them and not us."

"What do you mean?"

"Well, there's a relief that it's not happening to us. It's similar to when a teacher calls on someone else when we don't know the answer. It's like we've escaped something bad but on a much bigger scale."

"You think I'm happy that LB is dying?"

"That's not what I said. I'm saying that there is a feeling that the odds of survival have just increased for you. Like death has a quota and you've been spared." She looked over at me. "Even if it doesn't make any sense, even if that fellow patient is a very dear friend. I want you to know that those thoughts are common. It's part of our survival instincts."

"I would never think that!" I said, but the truth was that I did.

Dr. Maitlin sat upright. "Rell, you should be aware that LB's condition may also trigger some symptoms in you. You may experience phantom symptoms. Have you had any night sweats?"

"No."

"Loss of appetite?"

"No."

"No new nodes?"

I shook my head. It wasn't really a lie.

"So you have no symptoms." It was half a question, half a statement.

In the shower that morning I felt the slightest pea of a node in my neck. But when I fluttered my fingers over it, I decided it was a vein. "No. No symptoms."

From nowhere tears came.

"What's the matter, Rell?"

The tears were dripping off my chin.

"Rell?" She waited.

"I'm afraid I'm going to die."

Dr. Maitlin cupped her hands around mine, not firmly, but as if she were holding an injured bird, and then she pulled them away from my face. I smelled her perfume and felt the warmth of her breath. She held my hand firmer. "It's all part of the healing, Rell."

"But what if my cancer comes back?" I said.

"Then we'll deal with it. One step at a time."

The next morning before school I watched Ajax twist and turn, scratching his back against the grass in the back yard. His biggest concerns in life were stray cats and an occasional flea. Wouldn't it be great to go through life as a dog? Just roll around in the dirt all day. No parents. No homework. No worries. No school.

That day in English class, Mr. Meyers returned our poems. He wrote on mine, "Your work shows extreme maturity and depth of feeling. Would you mind sharing it with the class?"

I didn't want to be mature. I wanted to be a dog chasing geckos through the ginger. I tried to pay attention, but I kept thinking about LB.

During History class Frank Acoba pivoted his notebook to Paul Cruz. He had drawn a naked butt with "No one listens to you until you fart" written across it.

I smiled when I saw it.

Mr. Fields smiled back at me.

I'm not smiling at you. Why would I smile at you? Because you gave me such a terrific welcome my first day back at school? I don't think so. What about your blockbuster lectures? No, that's not it either.

Paul Cruz flashed his sketch of a naked woman straddling a motorcycle. When I saw it, my first thought was that he drew the woman without any scars. Everyone I knew at Stanhope had at least one scar.

At lunchtime I couldn't focus. I felt like I was drifting.

"Rell, are you with me?" Emi's voice sounded far away.

I wanted her to leave me alone. I wanted to keep floating. I was at Stanhope watching LB asleep in her bed.

"Rell, do you want to go?" Emi shoved the invitation in my face. "A Garden Show of Prom Gowns" at Neiman Marcus. "It's free," she said.

Mary, Mary, quite contrary, how does your garden grow?

The invitation had a border of sunflowers and daisies with orange butterflies fluttering through a vine.

With dreams of hell and cancer cells that's how my garden grows.

"It might be fun," she said.

My garden is full of weeds.

"Rell?"

I kept floating.

"Rell!" Emi grabbed my shoulders.

I opened my eyes. I wasn't in the cafeteria. I was in the school health room. The dragon was scratching at the window. He wanted to come in.

"Rell." It was my mother's voice.

"Come on, Sweetheart, let's get in the car." Dad was holding me up.

"Rell." It was Dr. Maitlin. "Do you know who I am?"

Of course, I know who you are.

"Do you know where you are?"

Doctors, nurses, metal beds. I'm in a hospital.

"Rell, I'm Dr. Yim."

I'm falling down a hole.

"You're going to feel a small sting, Rell," the doctor said. Another injection.

Can't you see me? I'm right here.

"This should keep her calm for the night," he said.

I'm falling.

Dad was there. He had his arm around Mom.

Dad, catch me.

When I awoke, Dr. Maitlin was sitting next to my bed reading. She looked up. "How are you doing, Rell?" She closed her book.

I struggled to smile.

"You had a rough day yesterday," she said.

I looked around the room. She was the only one there.

"Your parents went to the cafeteria to get some breakfast. I'll get them," she said.

I didn't answer.

"Rell, I'm going to call the nurse to stay with you while I go to the cafeteria."

"No." My voice sounded like an echo.

"I don't want to leave you alone."

"Stay." I closed my eyes, and as soon as I did, the falling started again. It was like I was drifting down, through the mattress, through the floor, down into somewhere I couldn't describe.

"Can you stay with me until they get back?" I asked.

"Sure," she said. "Just let me have them paged."

I stared at the ceiling as she made her call. The ceiling tiles around the air conditioning vent were gray.

When Dr. Maitlin got off the phone I asked, "What happened to me yesterday?"

"You passed out in the cafeteria," she said.

I remembered the dragon scratching at the screen. "Were there lots of kids around?"

"Emi was with you. And another friend who got the school nurse."

"How did I get to the health room?"

"By the time the nurse got to you, you had already come to and you walked to her office. No one saw anything more than that."

Everybody saw me.

I turned my face away from her, pushing my cheek into the pillow labeled "Honolulu General Hospital."

"Was anybody else there?"

"I don't know," she answered.

I hoped Nate wasn't there.

I curled myself around my pillow, keeping my back to Dr. Maitlin. "Was I crying?"

"No one mentioned that," she said. "Why do you think

you were crying?"

I drew in a big breath before I answered her. "It was LB." I paused. "All day long I kept seeing her. I'd get flashes of her. I'd be walking down the hall or in class, and I'd see her lying in her bed."

Dr. Maitlin rubbed my back, lightly, in small circles, like my mother used to do when I was young.

"The last thing I remember I was in the cafeteria and I was looking down at LB. It was like I was a camera mounted on the ceiling of her room, then I zoomed in closer and closer. She was dying. Then the camera moved right to her face. It was out of focus." I sobbed. "When it got clear I looked at the face. And it wasn't LB, it was me." I gripped my pillow harder. "I was in her bed." I cried. "I'm the one. I'm going to die, not her."

"Rell, LB is your best friend."

The door swung open. A doctor walked in, followed by Mom and Dad. They looked scared. Parents aren't supposed to get scared. They're supposed to make things better.

The doctor's nametag read "Donald Y.S. Yim, Chief of Psychiatric Services." He read over my chart, made a few notes and turned to me. "You gave us quite a scare, young lady." As if I did it on purpose. Then he turned to Dr. Maitlin. "Are you doing the follow up, Jeanne?"

She nodded.

"Family sessions?" he asked.

"Starting this week," she answered.

"All of us?" I asked.

"Uh-huh." She smiled.

I was afraid she'd tell Mom and Dad what I told her.

"Could I see all of you in the hall, please?" Dr. Yim asked.

Mom and Dad exchanged glances.

"Mr. and Mrs. DeMello." Dr. Yim gestured toward the door.

"We will be right there, doctor," Dad said, and he and Mom walked toward me. Mom kissed my head and brushed her hand over my cheek. Her eyes were red, her mouth drawn, and she smelled like cigarettes. "I love you, Sweetheart."

"How are you, Sunshine?" He held my hand.

"Just great," I said.

"You've had a tough year," Dad said.

"But I'm tough." I said it because I knew it was what he wanted to hear.

"We will be right outside that door, Rell. If you need us, just whistle." He gave me a wink.

"We love you," Mom said.

"I love you both, very much," I said.

Mom patted my hand and the two of them walked out. While they were all out in the hall talking, I got up and sneaked a look at my chart.

Dr. Maitlin wrote, "Possible post-traumatic stress episode. Intensive therapy and family sessions recommended."

Dr. Yim scribbled, "Normal adolescent reaction."

Normal? I couldn't find normal if I had a life-sized map.

I wasn't released until almost four o'clock in the afternoon. There were paperwork problems. There were always paperwork problems.

On the way home Dad sped through a yellow light.

Mom didn't yell. Both of them chatted about the local news, the weeds in the yard, the electric bill and a possible summer vacation—anything but just what happened.

We pulled into the driveway. Dad opened the car door for me and Mom held my elbow as I walked. She got me settled in my room, lined up extra pillows on my bed and brought in my dinner on the breakfast tray that Dad and I bought her for Mother's Day when I was in third grade.

After dinner I fell off to sleep until I heard them fighting. It was Mom's voice that woke me. "Why can't your commute from Hilo?" she said.

Dad said, "You know what the beginning of a job is like. I don't work a neat forty-hour week, Maria."

"I can't handle this by myself," Mom said.

I folded my pillow around my head to block out their words.

"What do you want me to do? Quit my job and stay home and watch you wallow in depression?"

"That's not fair, David. You just use work to hide."

There was a slam of a fist on the table.

"Run away, David. It's what you do best."

"Somebody has to pay the bills," Dad yelled.

"Just what that mean?"

"All your pay goes to Chinese herbs and cancer books and that damn psychologist."

"We need to talk to her, David."

"I don't need to pay to hear my wife whine. I get enough of that for free."

Please stop fighting.

"Damn it, David. You need her more than the rest of us."

"What I need is a wife who can handle things."

"The Great David DeMello! You don't need to talk to anyone. You can take care of everything yourself!" Mom was screaming. "There's nothing the Great David DeMello can't do!"

"I don't need to sit around and cry about my life. I'm the only one in this family who's not falling apart."

Daddy, do you think I'm falling apart?

"Don't ever say that, David. Don't you even think it."

I pretended not to hear. I flew away—down the steps of an oak-stained staircase. I held on to the rail and lifted my feet and I flew. The staircase switched back twice down to a landing with Chinese carpets and velvet chairs, and I flew until it was morning.

When I woke up the next morning a bouquet of pink anthurium had already been delivered to the house. The card read, "To my Estrella, My Most Beautiful Star. I love you, Dad."

Nothing but the best for his Estrella.

Mom was at the breakfast table reading the paper. She had her cell phone right next to her coffee mug.

"Morning, Mom."

"Good morning, Sweetheart." She kissed me. She had been smoking.

"What can I make you for breakfast?" She was already getting up and headed to the refrigerator.

"Cereal and orange juice is fine." I got a bowl out of the cupboard and a glass for the juice that she already had on the counter.

As she started to pour the juice I put my hand over hers.

"I can do it, Mom."

"You're right," she said and went back to the table. "How are you feeling?" she asked.

"Fine."

"Emi called. You may want to give her a call later."

"I will."

"And Nate called several times."

"Okay." I didn't feel like talking to anyone. "Do you have any plans for today?" I asked.

"There's a sale on at Marsh's," she said. "Jeans are half-price." She opened the paper up to show me. The ad was highlighted in a yellow. Mom couldn't read without a pen and a highlighter in her hand. She had to mark and grade everything like it was one of her students' papers.

"What time do we see Dr. Maitlin?" I asked.

"Eleven-thirty."

"Is Dad going to be there?" I asked.

"He can't make it. Work."

He doesn't want to make it—work.

"Do you think he'll ever go?" I asked.

Mom put the paper down. "I'm not sure, honey."

I sat down next to her.

"I'm sure if you asked him, he would go," Mom said.

"That's okay," I answered.

Mom sipped her coffee.

"Before we see Dr. Maitlin I want to ask you something," I began.

"Sure, honey."

"LB's not doing well." I knew she knew that already. "And I want to go to Stanhope to see her."

She didn't even flinch. She said, "I'll call Dr. Kosaki right now. I'm sure he will give me time off to go."

"I want to go by myself," I said.

She put down her coffee mug. She didn't answer. She just stared out the window at the jasmine and heliconia.

"Please, Mom."

She didn't answer me at first, then she said, "It's a long trip to make alone."

"It's not like the plane stops off in the middle of the ocean."

"You know what I mean, Rell."

"You could watch me board the plane at the airport and LB's parents will pick me up. It would be just for a few days. I'll be okay. Please."

"We have to talk to Dad," she said.

"But he'll listen to you," I said.

"When do you want to go?"

"This weekend if I can."

"Okay." She called Dad. Within an hour he had arranged for plane tickets for me, booked a limousine service to take me from the airport to Stanhope and reserved a room at Stanhope's Hospitality House. Making things happen is what Dad did best.

We didn't talk about it again until we were in the car on the way to Dr. Maitlin's office. Mom asked, "Are you sure you don't want me to go to San Francisco with you?"

"I'm sure."

"How are LB's parents doing?" she asked.

"I guess they're okay."

Mom kept her eyes on the road. "How bad is LB?" She

asked the question like she was asking one of her students about last week's lecture.

"I think she's dying," I answered.

We didn't talk for the rest of the trip. About a block from Dr. Maitlin's Mom stopped at Starbuck's for a cappuccino. She almost made us late. When she walked into the office Mom dumped the lid to her cappuccino in the trash. Dr. Maitlin took the lid off her latte, too. The whole office smelled like a Starbuck's.

I sat in my regular chair. Mom sat in a wooden chair with her back to the shelves of dinosaurs and monsters. She sat up straight with her feet on the floor. She had dark, puffy circles under her eyes.

Dr. Maitlin thanked Mom for coming, and before she laid out the rules about privacy she asked Mom, "Shall we wait for Mr. DeMello?"

"He won't be coming," Mom said. "He wanted to be here, but he was called back to the Big Island for an emergency."

Even Mom lies.

"He works long hours, doesn't he?" Dr. Maitlin echoed back to Mom.

"Yes. He's a project engineer." Mom held tight to her coffee cup.

"Well then, let's get started," Dr. Maitlin said.

"Fine," Mom answered.

Dr. Maitlin paused, like she was letting us catch our breath before we started up a steep climb. She looked at each of us then said to me, "Rell, do you know what happened at school the other day?"

"No."

"What do you think happened?"

Mom hunched over. She rested her elbows on her knees.

"I guess I passed out."

I could see a reflection of myself in Dr. Maitlin's glasses. I looked small and distorted. "Do you remember any particular feeling or any thoughts you were having that day?"

I didn't answer.

"Rell?" Dr. Maitlin said.

"I felt like I was falling down a hole," I said.

Mom sat motionless, hanging onto my every word.

"Could you see where the hole was?" Dr. Maitlin asked.

"It was in Alice's garden. But the Mad Hatter was in Peter Rabbit's garden." I felt foolish for saying it in front of Mom.

"What happened when you fell down the hole?" she asked.

"Nothing. I just kept falling."

"Did anything happen earlier that day? Did something upset you?"

She wants me to tell Mom about seeing myself in LB's bed.

"No."

"Do you want to take some time to think about your answer?"

"No."

"Okay." She understood. No more questions about that. She switched gears. "How are things going at home, Mrs. DeMello?"

Mom turned to me. "How do you think they are, Rell?"

"Actually, I'd like to hear your perspective," Dr. Maitlin said to Mom.

In a controlled voice Mom said, "Tense."

Dr Maitlin waited. Mom didn't volunteer anything more.

"In what way?" Dr. Maitlin asked.

"There's tension between Rell and me," she said.

What about between you and Dad?

"Can you be specific, Mrs. DeMello?"

"Rell doesn't take care of herself. She forgets to take her antibiotics. Sometimes she doesn't eat right. And she never uses sunscreen."

"That's not true," I said.

"She refuses to take vitamins," Mom added.

"They're not vitamins. They're herbs and you don't know what's in them."

"They're vitamins prescribed by a naturopath." Mom turned to Dr. Maitlin. "Everything is a battle when it comes to her health. She doesn't take care of herself."

"I take care of myself," I said.

Dr. Maitlin said to me, "Sometimes after a child or a teenager has had a life-threatening illness, parents react by becoming more watchful." Dr. Maitlin turned to Mom. "As parents we worry. We may become more strict. We may treat a teenager like a child. The rules in the house may get tighter or enforced more harshly. This is all very common."

Mom nodded.

"Under normal circumstances, it's hard enough for parents to figure out where the boundaries should be for your children. Where do we draw the line? How much freedom do we allow? But this is foreign territory. Mrs. DeMello, right now there are few role models for you to look toward." Then Dr. Maitlin addressed me. "It's hard on both of you."

Dr. Maitlin took a sip of her coffee. "Let's for a moment, consider a different scenario. Mrs. DeMello, what do you think would happen if you let Rell do anything she wanted to do?"

Mom pursed her lips tight, like she was holding straight pins in her mouth. She stared up at the poster of tropical fish on the wall opposite her. "She wouldn't take care of herself," she answered.

"I would, too," I said.

Dr. Maitlin looked over to me. I got quiet.

"How would she not take care of herself?" Dr. Maitlin asked.

Mom shook her head but didn't answer. I could see tears in her eyes.

"What about it, Rell?" Dr. Maitlin asked me. "Would you take your medication?"

"Yes."

"Do you take them everyday?" she asked.

"Most days, but sometimes I forget."

"How about your eating habits?"

"I eat!"

"Why does that question upset you?"

I said, "I'm not upset." But I could hear my teeth grind and feel my chest tense up.

Dr. Maitlin waited a bit, then she said to Mom, "Often with cancer patients, eating is the most common source of tension between the patient and their families—whether the patient is a parent and a child or a spouse." Dr. Maitlin continued, "The caregiver wants to see the patient eat because it makes them feel better. It's something they can do."

Mom nodded.

"Parents want to nurture their children. It's what we do. But teens want to be independent and return to normal life. So the battle often boils down to 'Eat' for a Mom and 'I don't want to' for the teen."

"It's more than the food," Mom said. "She does the opposite of whatever I ask. Sometimes to the point of being irresponsible."

"I am responsible, Mom."

"Give me some examples of how you're responsible, Rell." Dr. Maitlin said.

"I go to school. I get good grades." I looked at Mom. "Girls my age get pregnant. They do drugs. I know lots of kids who are drunk out of their minds every day at school. I am responsible, Mom."

"What else, Rell?" Dr. Maitlin asked.

"What more is there? I don't do drugs, except for chemo, and the only tattoos I have are from a radiation doctor."

"You're not careful, Rell," Mom said. "How many times have you forgotten your antibiotics?"

"Missing one pill isn't going to kill me, Mom."

"What if you get an infection?"

"I know what an infection feels like."

"You're supposed to take your antibiotic everyday."

"I do."

"You don't. You just said so."

"You don't care about me. You just want to catch me in a lie."

"I want to keep you alive, Rell!"

"By standing over me twenty four hours a day?"

"If I have to."

"You can't keep me alive, Mom."

"I can!"

"Tell her!" I screamed at Dr. Maitlin. "Nobody can keep me alive. She can't keep cancer away, not Dr. Braden, not me, nobody." The tears flowed. "Cancer doesn't care! Tell her."

It was like a bomb went off; then there was quiet. The dust had to settle, the cloud had to lift, then we could tally up who won and who lost and who was wounded in battle.

Mom thought she had a magic wand—one that could keep my cancer away. But there was no magic and she knew it. She saw kids at Stanhope with moms who tried to keep cancer away, but their kids died anyway.

I looked at Dr. Maitlin, afraid to make eye contact with my mother. "I told you before. She looks at me like I'm a cancer bomb waiting to go off."

"Talk to your mother, Rell. Not me. Explain what you feel."

"Sometimes I think you don't see me." I couldn't look at my mother so I stared down at my lap. "You see cancer. You stare at my neck where the cancer was." I looked up. "How would you like it if I stared at your chest all the time and asked you if you had breast cancer yet? Your mom had it and she died." I felt my heart pounding but I kept my voice under control.

"That's different, Rell."

"No, it's not." I tried to explain.

"I never had cancer," Mom said.

"Your mother had it and she died."

"That's different."

"No, it's not."

"I never had cancer," Mom said.

"How do you know you don't have it right now?"

God, why did I say that? But she didn't know. Nobody knows.

"I'm sorry, Sweetheart."

"And stop being sorry all the time!"

Another quiet.

I looked to Dr. Maitlin. "Tell her she can't keep the cancer away."

"Mrs. DeMello, do you believe you can control Rell's cancer?"

"I know I can't control her cancer, but I can control other factors. I can keep her more healthy and I can be more aware." Mom ran her fingers through her hair. "I can make sure she takes her antibiotics and gets plenty of rest."

"Mrs. DeMello, I'll ask again. Do you believe you can control Rell's cancer?"

Mom sighed. "When Rell first got sick I should have been more aware. If I had been, maybe things would have been different."

As she talked I studied the swirl in the carpet, from my chair to Dr. Maitlin's, from Dr. Maitlin's to Mom's.

"Mrs. DeMello, what do you mean that things would have been different?" Dr. Maitlin asked.

"I should have insisted on more tests. It took the doctors five months to diagnose her. When she was losing weight and her 'cold' went on for a month, I should have forced them to look for something more serious. Maybe she would have only been a Stage I and she would not have had to have both chemo and radiation."

"Do you think it was your fault that Rell was diagnosed so late?" she asked.

"I don't know," Mom said.

Dr. Maitlin took off her glasses. "The very sad truth is that we all treat doctors as if they were gods. And as gods they are supposed to be infallible. So, when they are wrong, our trust in the entire medical system erodes. We're like children who find out their parents aren't perfect."

"But maybe things would have been different," Mom said.

Dr. Maitlin looked at me then at Mom. "Each of you loves each other very much." She settled her eyes on me. "You both know that."

I gave a slight nod.

"But what you have to do now is to learn how to trust each other in ways you never had to before. This is all new for you. Rell, that means that your mother has to know with deep certainty that you are not putting your health in jeopardy. She has to know that you will tell her if something—anything—is bothering you. As a parent, she has the right to know that. And Mrs. DeMello, you have to begin to let go and let Rell take responsibility for herself."

"But," Mom interrupted her.

"Please let me finish," Dr. Maitlin said. "Rell tells me that she wants to go away to college."

"How can I let her go away when … ," Mom interrupted again.

"Please, Mrs. DeMello."

Mom sat back.

"The question you should be asking isn't, 'How can I allow her to go away to college?' but rather, 'How can I prepare her to live independently?' That means giving her the opportunity to make her own choices and trusting that she will do the right thing. And she will make mistakes along the way. It's all part of the learning. And that's how trust will be built up between you—slowly."

Mom nodded.

Dr. Maitlin said, "I have an assignment for both of you. For the next few days I want you both to pretend that Rell is on vacation from cancer. Mrs. DeMello, I want you to pretend that Rell is not at risk for anything, not even a cold. When you feel yourself wanting to protect her, stop and say to yourself, 'Just for today, cancer is not part of my life.' Is that a deal?"

Mom agreed.

"There will be no discussion of cancer unless Rell brings it up." She looked at Mom. "It also means that if Rell does something she should be punished for, you punish her. There will be no special food, no special curfew, no decisions based on her medical history."

Then she looked to me. "That also means no asking for special privileges, no getting out of any chores, no bids for sympathy with anyone at school or at home. Got it?"

"Yes."

"And remember, Rell, you have to be honest with your mother. If you have any symptoms, any concerns or questions about your health, you must talk to her about it."

"Okay."

On the ride home Mom and I didn't speak to each other. We didn't look at each other. It was as if we had seen each other naked in the locker room and we were too embarrassed to face each other again.

CHAPTER EIGHT

Later that day I checked my neck in the mirror. The tiny pea was still there. I took out a pen and rolled it over the node, just like Dr. Braden had taught me. Then I measured the line. It was less than an eighth of an inch long.

"Cancer feels like a hard pea." That's what Dr. Braden said. "And it doesn't move."

I rolled my finger over it. I tried to push it up and down. I squeezed it between my fingers. It wouldn't move.

I flushed hot. I couldn't breathe. I sat on my bed and began to cry. At first it was just a whimper, then muffled sobs. I cried loud enough for my mother to hear me, for her to come in my room and cradle me and wrap her arms around me and rock me and kiss me and make me all better.

She kissed the top of my scalp. She rocked me and spread her arms around me.

"It's not fair," I said. "It's not fair.

"You're right, Sweetheart. It's not fair," she said, and she held me until my cries became sobs, then whimpers then silent tears.

"I hate cancer," I said.

"I know," she said. "But LB may be hitting a bad time."

I let her think I was crying about someone else. "Sometimes, I get so afraid," I said.

"Rell, don't give up hope." She reached over for a tissue and wiped my face.

"I won't."

"Sometimes I get afraid for myself."

I said it.

"That's to be expected. Everything is still so fresh. In a few years, when there are no more tests, it'll be easier. It'll be easier on all of us."

That didn't make me feel any better.

"In the meantime, once you get back to school, back on the debate team...."

"I don't want to go back to school," I interrupted her.

"You don't have to go back right away. We can wait until you get back from Stanhope." She stroked my cheek.

"I mean I don't ever want to go back. Ever."

"Rell, you have to go back to school."

"I could transfer—go to Oahu Academy for Girls. Dad always wanted me to go to a girls' school."

"Rell."

"Please, Mom. I can't ever go back there."

"This isn't a decision to make lightly," she said.

"Please."

"The three of us need to talk about this, not just Dad and I," she said. "In fact, it may be something we should all talk about with Dr. Maitlin."

"I can't face going back. Not after everybody saw me. I can't."

Mom held me for a little longer. "Rell, you are such a strong woman. You're a lot strong than you think." She let go and leaned back. "I wish my mother were alive to see you. She'd be so proud."

My Grandmother Toni died when I was eight.

"She was such an elegant lady, Rell—just like you. And the way you've handled this disease." Mom's eyes welled up. "I'm not sure I could have handled it as well." She tried to smile. "You come from good stock." She joked.

"Yes. A good line of Cabral and DeMello women who had babies in the field and went right back to baking bread."

"And before they went to bed at night, they chopped wood for the ovens."

But I was still afraid.

"And do you know what else the Cabral and DeMello women are famous for?" Mom patted my hand. "Making their daughters hearty suppers."

"Mom!"

She held up her watch. "It's six o'clock. Supper-talk is fair, even under Dr. Maitlin's rules," she said.

"Rell, did you call Emi back?"

I shook my head. "I'll call her tonight."

"And Nate called about ten minutes ago."

"Okay," I said. I just wanted Nate to go away.

That's what is was like. I was afraid, and then I'd get distracted. But the fear never totally went away, and when Mom went back into the kitchen, my hand went directly to my neck. My whole future depended on one small-as-a-pea, not-moving node.

The next morning the node seemed smaller. Or maybe I just wanted it to be. I took a shower and soaped up my neck and slithered my fingers over the node at least ten times. It was smaller, I was sure of it.

I was happy until I emailed LB. Her X-rays confirmed that she had pneumonia and her nosebleeds were getting worse. She was worried about her parents, too. They were taking a lot of time off from work to be with her. Both of LB's parents worked at a computer assembly plant. Sometimes on weekends her dad made extra money as a bartender. Once, right after she got diagnosed, the plant had a cake sale to help them pay for the medical bills.

LB wrote, "It would be easier for them if I died."

"Don't even think that, LB."

"But it would."

"They would do the same thing for your brother. And you'd probably get a job to help them out."

"That's different."

"No, it's not. You know you would never give up on your brother."

"I'm tired, Rell. I better go."

"What about your blood test?"

"I've got to go, Rell."

"LB, please don't think dying would be easier than treatment."

"I'm tired, Rell."

There was no way to keep her online.

"I love you, LB," I wrote.

"Right back at you, Roomie," she answered.

Mom was on the phone when I got to the kitchen. "Yes, Dr. Kosaki," she exaggerated his name as she spoke to let me know it was her boss on the phone. "She's much better. Thank you for asking." She took out some leftover lasagna from the fridge. Ajax sat right next to her, begging. "Yes," she said. "I'll be back to work on Monday." She cradled the phone against her collarbone as she took two pieces out and put them on a plate.

I got the dishes and glasses out of the cupboard. "Thanks," she mouthed to me then she went back to her conversation. "Absolutely," she said. "Don't change any of my appointments, I will be there." There was a pause. Then she said, "Thank you. I'll see you then." She hung up the phone and shoved the lasagna in the microwave.

"Does the whole world know what happened to me?" I asked.

"The school nurse left a message for me while I was in a faculty meeting. All Dr. Kosaki knows is that you got sick." She got the lettuce out of the fridge. "Do you want tomatoes and olives in your salad?"

"Please," I said.

"Remember to call back Emi and Nate. Okay?"

Why was she obsessed with me calling back my friends?

"Faye and Sharlene called, too. And Sarah dropped by."

I didn't want to talk to anyone. LB was dying, I passed out, and I had a node in my neck I was trying to convince myself was getting smaller.

"You okay, Rell?" Mom asked.

"Yes."

After dinner I called Emi. Her first question was, "Are you okay?"

"I'm fine," I said.

"Really okay?"

"Yes."

"What happened?"

"I thought you could tell me."

"I was talking to you and you started staring at the ceiling.

Then your eyes rolled up and you passed out on the table."

"You mean on the table? Into my food?"

"No. You knocked over my soda, but you missed everything else," she said. "Then Faye ran for the school nurse and Nate and I stayed with you. By the time the nurse got to the cafeteria you already came to and walked into her office."

"Nate was there?"

"He kept kids away."

"Were there crowds around me?"

"Not really—well, maybe for a few seconds. But after you came to, nobody paid attention."

"Did they send an ambulance for me?"

"No, Miss High Drama. Your parents picked you up."

"But everybody saw me."

"Rell, the whole thing took five minutes. Most kids probably thought you were drugged out."

"You know that's not true."

"Okay, it's not true. But, it wasn't as bad as you think," Emi said.

"And Abe Lincoln never told a lie."

"It was George Washington who never lied," she corrected me.

"I'll never be able to go back to school now," I said.

"Don't flatter yourself. By Monday you'll be old news."

"I won't be there on Monday. I'm going to San Francisco to see LB." I paused. "She's really sick."

"Is she dying?"

"No." I was afraid that if I said yes, I might make it come true.

"Have you told Nate you're going?" she asked.

"I haven't talked to him."

"He said he calls your house all the time," Emi said. "Rell, he's really a nice guy and he likes you a lot."

"Since when are you one of his biggest fans?"

"When you sit around a hospital waiting room with someone for seven hours you run out of small talk fast."

"Nate was at the hospital, too?"

"He drove me over and we stayed until your parents told us to go home. I think he's great, Rell."

"What about the stuff your brother said about him?"

"My brother's a jerk. He probably made the whole thing up," she said.

"Maybe not."

"You should call Nate."

"I will. As soon as we get off the phone," I said. But I knew I wouldn't do it.

"Then I'll hang up now so you can call."

"You call him for me."

"What?"

"You call, Emi. Please."

"Why?"

"I can't talk to him," I said. "I don't know if I can ever face him again."

"That's ridiculous."

"Please, Emi."

"This is beginning to reek of Sweet Valley High."

"If you don't call, I won't," I said. "I just can't."

"What do you want me to say?"

"Can you ask him to come over tomorrow night but

not call me or anything until then?"

"Any more rules?"

"Not to ask me about what happened."

"Rell, I was kidding. I'll call him but I'm not going to tell him what he can or can't say."

"But you will call?"

"Yes."

"I owe you for this, Emi."

"You owe me big," she said.

Friday morning I didn't roll out of bed until nine o'clock. Mom was potting oregano next to the barbecue pit. I slid the patio glass door open. "I thought you had a student conference this morning," I said.

Mom was wearing one of Dad's old undershirts, translucent with sweat. "I did, but my student cancelled." She put down the pot and wiped the sweat from her face with her forearm and bent back from her waist, rubbing the bottom of her spine. "It's tough getting old." She smiled. "Come on out here and talk to me," she said. "I need a break."

"Let me get a bowl of cereal and I'll be out."

I juggled my cereal bowl, my glass of juice and a mug of coffee for Mom. I made it to the chairs without spilling a drop, despite Ajax herding me toward the patio. Mom lifted three more pots onto the tiled counter next to the grill. "Slugs! They're chewing up my basil. Look."

"Mrs. Zoller says that if you put beer in the saucer they'll be attracted to it and drown."

Mom angled the herb pot to the sun. I could see the

gelatinous trail shining up and over the Koolau Nursery price tag.

"I hate slugs," she said.

Mom dragged two chairs under the shade of the mango tree. "Right after I finish up, I'm going to Safeway and buy beer and I'm going to put it in every plant saucer I have." She pointed to the cleared herb garden beside the canvas swing. "I dug out all the mint this morning. It was taking over."

"It looks like you got carried away," I said.

"It'll grow back." She took off her garden gloves, exposing clean, pink hands at the end of dirt-veiled arms. She took a sip of her coffee. "I was thinking of planting night-blooming jasmine in that corner for you," she said. "This way you could smell it from your room at night."

"Is that a special privilege, or do you think that Dr. Maitlin will allow it?" I asked.

"I think plants are within the rules," she said.

"What do you think of Dr. Maitlin?" I asked.

"She's certainly effective." Mom looked over and raised her eyebrows as if to say, "Look what happened yesterday." Mom continued, "You know, Sweetheart, I wouldn't ask you so many questions if you would talk to me more."

"I know."

"You want to try talking now?" she asked.

"Maybe another time," I said.

"What if I go first?" Mom put her coffee mug down. "Trust Building 101." She took in a deep breath. "Rell, you were right when you told Dr. Maitlin that I'm afraid that you'll get sick again. I know that you have nightmares about it, but I have nightmares, too." She glanced over at me. "I have one recurring nightmare where I'm an old lady, kind of a troll, really, complete with a curved spine and a mole on my nose." She hunched over and rounded her shoulders. "I'm standing on the bridge of a castle, guarding the moat entrance, making sure that the dragon doesn't attack." She took another sip of her coffee and held the mug close to her chest. "I don't eat. I don't sleep. All I do is guard the castle." Tears filled her eyes, finding their way deep into her crow's feet. "I have a weapon in my hand but I can't see what it is. But, still, I am poised for battle. I stand there, day after day, watching for the dragon. If there is the slightest wind in the trees or the rustle of an animal through the woods, I aim my weapon. But," she wiped her tears with the corner of her T-shirt, "I never looked up." She shrugged slightly. "Then my view zooms out and I see myself pacing on the bridge. Overhead, the dragon is circling. He swoops low, dives toward the castle turret with his talons stretched out and scoops up the princess and flies away." She looked at me with a forced smile. "It doesn't take a psychologist to interpret that dream."

She's afraid of the dragon, too.

"So, you want to know why I make such a fuss about sunscreen and antibiotics? It's because I forgot to look up."

"Maybe we're all supposed to be watching out, Mom, not just you."

"But I'm your mother."

"You are a great mother," I said. "And if I were a dragon I wouldn't want to go up against you." I tried to lighten up the conversation.

"Am I that bad?" Mom asked.

"You breathe fire." I laughed.

"Sorry," she said.

"Mom, in your dreams, do I have long, flowing blonde hair?"

"No, Miss Rapunzel, in my dream you are as beautiful as you are right now."

I fingered my stubbly locks. "Do me a favor, the next time you're dreaming, could you give me long hair?"

"No," she said. "I love you just the way you are."

After breakfast I called Emi. I sat on the edge of my bed and cradled the phone in my ear while I was getting dressed.

"An all-girls' school? Are you crazy?" Emi wasn't exactly supportive of the idea of transferring to Oahu Academy.

"Nobody would know me there." I squeezed the phone to my ear with my shoulder while I zipped my jeans. They were tight. I was gaining more weight back.

"Rell, it's a small island. Somebody would know you."

"But not at first."

"You're right, for the first two days you'd be safe," she said. "Rell, there are girls from all over the island at the academy—including Kailua. And at least one of them would know Miss Oahu-Academy-Wannabe Wanda."

"You're right," I admitted.

"I'm always right," Emi said.

"Maybe I could transfer to the moon," I said.

"No good," she said. "Some auntie would have a cousin, whose son is an astronaut assigned to moon patrol."

"Hold on," I said as I tossed the phone on the bed and slipped my *Dreamcatcher* shirt on over my head. "I'm never going back to school. I can't face anyone again."

"Not even Nate?"

"What did he say when you called him?"

"He said he'd be there at five."

And at precisely at five, the doorbell rang. I adjusted my wig and answered the door. Mom got to it first. She hugged Nate. I never saw her hug him. I wasn't sure I was happy about it, either. When they saw me with a wig on, both of them stared at my head.

"Hi," I said.

Nate brought me a bouquet of sunflowers tied with a raffia. I hugged him, maybe he hugged me, I'm not sure. We were both tense, I could feel it.

"You're looking good, Rell." He gave me a thumbs up. I remembered the first time he did that in the mall parking lot.

"Thanks."

Nate looked so strong—square-jawed, sharp-eyed.

Enter fantasy: I'm skipping though a field of sunflowers. My hair is trailing behind me. I'm in slow-motion. A breeze clings to my body. I run to Nate with my arms extended. He lifts me in the air and we twirl forever.

Enter reality: I didn't know what to say.

"Are you two going out, or can I entice you to stay home with me and watch a video?"

Nate and I exchanged glances. "Definitely out," we answered together.

"How about Gino's for dinner?" he asked.

"A booth in the back, a table in the dark." It was a line from a movie that I could never get straight.

When we got to Gino's the hostess seated us at a table next to the street-side window.

Nate pulled out my chair. He was my dashing prince in

ironed, creased jeans and a black-knit collared shirt. "You do look terrific," he said.

I contorted my lips into a smile. I pictured him sitting in the hospital waiting room with Emi, talking and leafing through two-year-old magazines and watching CNN on TV.

"Do you know what you want?" he said.

"In the big scheme of life, or just tonight?" I said.

"Just dinner for right now." Nate read over his menu. As he did, I glanced across the street toward the bowling alley. A family was unfolding themselves out of a minivan. Like ducks in a line with bowling bags for wings, they waddled through the parking lot to the front door.

When I looked back at Nate, he was staring at my wig.

"I didn't want any extra attention tonight. Passing out at school was enough for a lifetime."

"Rell, it wasn't that bad."

Sure, right in the middle of the red-bean chili, there was my face splattered with ground beef and onions.

"The waitress is coming." Nate folded over his menu.

"You ready to order?" She pulled her order pad out of her skirt band. Nate ordered lasagna.

"Me too," I said. I didn't want to have to make any choices.

"Anything to drink?"

"Diet Coke," I answered.

"And two glasses of water," Nate added.

Nate and I held hands across the table, flanking an unlit candle stuffed in a straw-covered Chianti bottle.

"I'm sorry," I said. It seemed like I was always apologizing.

"For what?"

"I don't know. For Wednesday, I guess."

"Let it go, Rell."

I leaned back as the busboy poured our water. His shirt smelled like fried garlic, and he could have used some deodorant.

"My Mom said you were at the hospital until midnight."

"I stayed for a while."

"I'm sorry." I couldn't stop saying it.

"Forget it, Rell. Move on."

Maybe it was a guy thing. You don't say you're sorry. You blow the winning shot. Your team loses the state championship. You don't fall to your knees and cry. You don't change your name and move to a different city. You don't even drown yourself in a gallon of ice cream. You just let it go. You forget it. You move on.

"I'll try," I said.

"Your mom said you're going to Stanhope to see LB."

I didn't like it that he talked to my mother. "Uh-huh."

"Your mother is worried about how you'll react."

I pulled my hands back.

"She thinks she should go with you," Nate said. "She's worried about you."

That was it. "My mother cannot live without worrying. It's like breathing to her."

"She's your mother."

I folded my arms across my chest.

"Before you go I want to tell you something."

I wasn't in the mood to hear anything he was going to say. I couldn't handle any news—good, bad or indifferent. For one night I wanted everything to stay the same, no changes, no promises and no great revelations.

"If it's that you're the son of a Texas billionaire, I already know," I said.

I caught the guy at the next table eavesdropping on us. He was about forty, overweight with eight strands of gray hair combed over his glaring scalp. When he caught me looking at him he turned away.

"Not even close," Nate said.

"Lasagna." The waitress put a plate down in front of me. "And lasagna." She put the second plate down in front of Nate.

I reached for the bread basket.

"Your Mom told me you're leaving at one tomorrow."

"Did she tell you my seat number, too?" I was wondering what else my mother told him about me.

"Would you mind if I went to the airport to see you off?" Nate asked.

"I would mind if you didn't."

A gray-haired woman, thick-bodied in a too-tight business suit, walked into the restaurant. The bald man at the next table stood up. The two of them politely embraced.

I took a few bites of lasagna and looked out the window, wondering if the minivan family were good bowlers. They probably owned bowling shoes. I rested my elbow on the table, and without any thought, my fingers were seesawing over the small round pea still in my neck.

"Something wrong?" Nate stared at my hand.

"No." I immediately reached for my Coke.

"You sure?"

"Yes, I am sure."

"I've been reading about Hodgkin's disease," he said.

"Why? Are you studying for a Hodgkin's test I don't know about?"

"No, I just wanted to know more about you."

"I am not about cancer." I tried to keep my voice low.

"Okay." He glanced around the room. "I wanted to know more about you, and what you went through." He huddled in closer. "You—a cancer surivior."

"I am not a cancer survivor," I said.

Nate tensed. He sat straighter. "Rell, you had cancer, you were treated and you survived that makes you a cancer survivor." Cold-hearted logic from the mathematics tutor. "It's nothing to be ashamed of," he said.

"I'm not an anything survivor. I'm just like anybody else except I had cancer."

"So did I." Nate put his hand out to introduce himself. "Nate Lee, T-cell lymphoma, Stage II, seventy weeks treatment."

I felt like I did when I fell off the monkey bars on the playground and I got the wind knocked out of me and I couldn't breath and I sucked in air until I filled my lungs and panted and cried and lay there until the teacher ran over and picked me up.

"That's what I wanted to tell you," he said.

Somewhere deep inside my gut, I always knew it.

"The waitress stopped by with a tall wooden cheese grater. "Is everything all right here?" she asked.

"Just perfect," I answered.

"T-cell lymphoma. Stage II. Seventy weeks of treatment."

Neither of us looked up. We both sat, moving our food around on the plate, not eating.

"I'm sorry," Nate said.

"You say you're sorry when you bump into someone, or

you step on their toe, not when you forget to tell them you had cancer."

"I meant to tell you before," Nate said.

And I meant to be Miss America.

"The time was never right," he said.

I will not cry. I thought about Ajax chasing his tail, I remembered the magician at Emi's tenth birthday party, my ladybug costume for Halloween, my first bra, my first period, the first time I plucked my eyebrows. I tried to think of anything except the fact that I had a boyfriend, or I didn't have a boyfriend, who once had cancer and never got around to telling me.

"How could you not tell me?" My tears came.

"I wanted to. Honest."

I straightened my back and tried not to look embarrased while I felt tears dripping off my jaw. The busboy came by to fill our glasses, but after a quick look at my face, he kept walking. I put down my fork and used my napkin as a tissue. "I think we should go."

Nate paid the check and we left. We walked through the parking lot to his rust-bucket truck and sat under the glaring yellow light like two contestants in a game show booth, rigidly staring straight ahead, not daring to make eye contact with the other.

"I tried to tell you."

"You lied to me," I said.

"I didn't lie."

"You knew I had cancer."

"Everybody knew."

"But I didn't know about you. You lied."

"It's not something I broadcast."

"Why not?"

He didn't answer the question. He said, "I didn't want you to feel sorry for me."

"But you had the right to feel sorry for me?"

"What did you want me to do? Say, 'Hi, I'm Nate Lee, I've had cancer. Do you want to go out?' Would you have gone out with me if you knew?"

I could just hear the rumors at school. Nate and Rell, the Cancer Couple. "Probably not," I said.

"I didn't think so."

"But you didn't give me a chance to decide."

"I was afraid you'd say no, then once we started to go out I was afraid to tell you."

"Why did you want to go out with me in the first place? Was it because I was sick?"

"I don't know."

"Emi used to say that you went out with me to protect me. Is that true?"

"Maybe at first."

I wanted my words to come out in a hundred different directions. I wanted to ask and to explain and know and listen all at the same time. I wanted Nate to tell me what I wanted to hear, but none of it happened and his answers weren't exactly right.

"Is cancer the reason you transferred from St. Luke's?"

"Part of it."

"But there must be guys at school who know about it."

Nate scraped dirt off the steering wheel with his fingernail. "Guys are different," he said. "At first they may treat you differently, but once you're on the court and you get in a few good shots—you shove them, they shove you—it's over. Nobody cares."

"Basketball?"

"I'm just saying that guys get over things. Their friends don't make an issue of things."

"Cancer's a girl thing? You mean all this time all I had to do was shoot some hoops and it all goes away?" I threw my hands up in the air. "It was that easy and you never told me."

"Rell, guys are different."

"Yes. Mr. Rogers explained it. Guys are prettier on the outside."

Nate was drumming the steering wheel. "I didn't say I forgot it ever happened to me. I just don't think about it a lot."

I turned to him and asked. "Okay, how do you do that?"

"I keep it in a box," he answered.

Move on. Get over it. Keep it in a box.

"I guess I don't have strong enough tape."

"Rell, I'm not saying I'm not changed. It changed me a lot."

"How?" I wasn't sure I wanted to know.

"I don't wait for things to happen, I make them happen and I do things the first time they come around. I take risks."

I turned to him. "You're not exactly a skydiving kind of guy."

"Calculated risks."

Of course, numbers. Everything with Nate could be reduced to numbers.

I took in a deep breath. "What kind of odds did your doctor give you?" I asked.

"She told me my cancer would probably never come back. But, she couldn't say 100 percent."

"And you never thought it was back?"

"I watch myself," he said. "If something is wrong, I see my doc."

"That simple."

He nodded.

"I don't believe you."

"Rell, if I looked for cancer, I could find it everyday." Nate leaned against the door and put his knee up on the seat. "I choose not to."

Liar. Liar. Pants on fire.

"When you were sick did you ever think about dying?" I asked.

"Sometimes."

"What did you think about?"

"How there were things I wanted to do—like teach my cousin Noah how to dribble."

"I've seen you dribble. You have nothing to teach him."

"But I give it all I've got." He smiled. "Tell me what you thought about."

"About how sad it would be for my mom and dad if I died, and I thought about all the things I would miss doing— like getting married and having a baby." I leaned my back on the door and faced him. "Truth or dare," I said to him.

"Truth."

"What do you think is stronger, hope or fear?"

"Whatever sees you through," he answered.

I pressed my finger on my neck. "Truth: I have a new node on my neck. It's small but it's hard and it doesn't move." I turned to him. "So, what's stronger, hope or fear?"

He slid over and and put his arm around me and we

hugged. "When did you find it?" he asked.

"A couple of days ago."

"What did the doctors say?"

"I haven't told anyone yet."

"Not even your parents?"

I raised my head. "You're the first to know."

"Rell, you know you have to get this checked."

I nodded.

"Right away," he said.

"I know."

"When are you going to make the appointment?" Nate was in his action mode.

"When I go to Stanhope I'm going to ask Dr. Braden to take a look at it," I said.

"What about your parents?"

"I'm not going to tell them," I said. "It could be nothing. I don't want them to worry."

"And you think a doctor is going to check you without telling your parents?"

"Dr. Braden will do it. He's a good guy."

CHAPTER NINE

At nine o'clock Sunday morning my mother came in my room. She sat on my bed and held my hand. I was sure she was going to tell me that LB died.

"Mrs. O'Donnell called. The doctor's aren't sure that LB is going to make it through the weekend," she said. "Dad changed your flight to this afternoon."

I called Emi's house and left a message on their machine. I knew no one would be home. Emi's family were church-going Methodists. We were Christmas and Easter Catholics. I asked her to come over as soon as she could.

By noon I had laid out all my clothes on my bed like cards in a solitaire game. I paired up my red metallic socks with my denim jumper, folded up my only winter coat, and was layering everything in my suitcase when Emi walked in. She was carrying a three-foot-long flower box of orchids, ti leaves and ginger and a box of chocolates.

"The flowers are from my parents for LB," she said. "And these are for her from me." She handed me a box of chocolate-covered macadamia nuts.

"Thanks." I hugged her. Her perfume smelled like strawberries and vanilla. "Can you give me a hand with this?" I asked, pointing at my suitcase.

Emi sat on my suitcase while I tried forcing the zipper closed. It wasn't working.

"Do you have a bigger suitcase?" she asked.

"No." I grunted. "And I don't want to take two."

She got up and I sat on the suitcase. I jammed my elbow on the edge and leaned my body into it until Emi tugged the zipper closed.

"Teamwork," Emi said.

"Best friends."

We hooked our pinkies together.

"I wish I could go with you," she said. "But I'm not sure what I could do." Emi hugged me. "I'm sorry, Rell."

"We've got to leave, Rell," Mom yelled from the kitchen.

Dad came in and took my bag, and Mom wrapped up her cream cheese brownies for Dr. Braden. On the ride to the airport nobody talked. Emi reached for my hand and gave it a tight squeeze.

Nate was waiting for us at the airport. The two of us walked hand-in-hand. "How are you doing?" he asked.

"It's going to be hard."

"You're tougher than you think, Rell."

Right. I come from a long line of tough Cabral and DeMello women.

"I'm not so sure."

"When it gets hard, think of LB," he said.

We walked over to the window and watched the planes. "Rell, promise me you'll get yourself checked."

I nodded. "I will."

"And take a notebook with you and write down every thing Dr. Braden says."

"I will."

"And call me if you get bad news."

"I will."

"You know this is serious."

I nodded.

"Is the node still there?"

"Uh-huh."

"It's probably just a reactive node," he said.

That wasn't a mathematical formula. That was Nate trying to be reassuring.

"I hope so," I said.

Then, right before I boarded the plane, with my parents standing right next to me, Nate kissed me. He kissed me—in front of my parents. It was only a peck on the cheek, but he kissed me with my parents watching. For the next five hours on the plane, I replayed the kiss.

When I arrived at the San Francisco airport, a limousine driver in the baggage-claim area held a cardboard sign reading "Rell DeMello" in big red felt tip letters. I felt like a corporate executive getting off the plane. I should have been carrying a laptop computer and attaché instead of a box of flowers and a zipper-screaming plaid suitcase.

The driver loaded my luggage into the car and drove me to Stanhope's Hospitality House.

The night clerk at the Hospitality House carried my bag and walked me down to my room. The room had two twin beds and a cot. Each was covered with a different printed bedspread. The bathroom had jumbles of donated hotel soap and the coffee table was stacked with old magazines. On the nightstand was a red vinyl binder filled with handwritten notes—tips and encouragement from families who stayed in the room before. It was just like the room that Mom and I stayed in while I was in treatment. I remembered unpacking that first night, hoping that my diagnosis was all a mistake and that the next morning the Stanhope doctors would take some tests and send me home.

I unpacked my bag and called LB's room.

Mrs. O'Donnell answered. "Rell, it's so great to hear your voice."

Her voice sounded weak, tired and filled with constant sighs. She apologized for not picking me up at the airport and asked if I was hungry. "I could have Mr. O'Donnell bring you over some food."

In some ways all cancer moms were the same—they all wanted to feed you. Mrs. O'Donnell told me, "LB looks different from when you last saw her. She's lost a lot of weight and she's in pain most of the time." She took in a long breath. "Last night she had a chest tube put in. She's on morphine." She took in another long breath and exhaled in bellows of long, rolling waves. "If it gets too hard for you to be here, Rell, we will all understand."

There was nothing to say.

"If you'd like to come over now, Mr. O'Donnell can walk over for you, but LB's probably asleep for the night."

"I'm kind of tired from the flight," I said. "I was going to just go to bed."

"Okay, honey. You call us in the morning and we'll come get you."

I hung up and took a shower. The node on my neck was bigger.

I sat on the bed leafing through a year-old *People*

magazine, looking at wedding photos of stars who were already divorced. I remembered how Mom set up our room when we were there. She put her computer on the dresser and built a bookshelf out of cinderblocks and shelving. She used the ironing board for her files. Mom taught three classes from there and tried to turn it into a home. I missed her. I looked over at the empty bed next to mine and wished she were there.

The next morning, I put on my yellow long-sleeve top and my Hat-Hair wig. I grabbed the chocolates and flowers and walked into Stanhope's East Wing, past the cafeteria and gift shop, past the florist, the barber and the post office. It was all so familiar—doctors being paged, deliverymen carrying bouquets. An orderly wheeled an elderly woman with a respirator into the elevator. I squeezed between them and the wall.

"Seventh floor, please," I said, knowing that the orderly knew that the seventh floor was the Pediatric Oncology Unit. I checked myself out in the smoked glass walls. I was happy I was wearing my wig and carrying Emi's flowers and candy. It made me look like a visitor and not a patient.

I got out on the seventh floor and turned left—I was back. At first I couldn't move. I just stood there. A Red Cross volunteer walked by and asked "Are you lost?"

"No." I shook my head.

I swung open the red iron "castle" gate and walked past the murals of kings and queens and the cutouts of wide-eyed deer and rabbits. Two boys raced down the hall on their plastic tricycles. Any second I knew a nurse would appear and put them on "time out."

I walked straight to the nurses' station and checked the patient board. "Elizabeth O'Donnell, Room 7-12." She was still in the same room.

I stood at the door.

I really don't want to do this.

I opened the door.

LB was asleep. Mr. O'Donnell turned to me and waved me in. "Rell." He got up and gave me a bear hug that almost lifted me off my toes. "Great to see you, kiddo." His beard bristled against my face. "You are quite the young lady," he said.

He let me go and I caught my balance.

"Let me take a good look at you."

I held the box of chocolates and flowers in the air and spun around.

"You look wonderful, kiddo." He pointed to the boxes. "Whatcha got there?" "Flowers from Hawai`i," I said. "They're from my friend's mom for LB.

"Hawaiian chocolates!" He took them from my hand. "You remembered."

I had forgotten how much Mr. O'Donnell liked them, but I said, "Yup. Special delivery just for you." I figured Emi wouldn't mind. Besides, she'd never know.

"Rell, it means so much to LB that you're here." Mr. O'Donnell looked tired. His cheeks had crease marks from the chair's pillow. He had bags under his eyes and his beard had a three-day growth.

"You look so healthy, Rell."

It made me feel guilty. I wanted to run away. "Let me get these flowers in water," I said, and I checked around in the bathroom cabinets for something to use as a vase. The smells—the bleached sinks, the Phisodex, the hospital-laundered towels. It all came back—the alcohol, the antiseptics, the wax on the floor.

I found a vase and put the flowers on LB's nightstand.

"Hi, Roomie," I heard LB say.

"Hi."

LB had lost more weight than I expected. Her cheekbones were hallowed and her eyes looked sunken.

Such big eyes you have, Grandma.

I dragged a chair next to her bed. I lifted the drainage tube from LB's chest over the back of the chair and I sat cross-legged with my elbows on my knees. The noise from the drainage tube was loud, like a giant robot slurping soda, and the fluid was cloudy.

Mr. O'Donnell moved to the foot of LB's bed. "Elizabeth, I'm going down to the cafeteria to let Mom know that Rell's here. Do you want anything, Baby?"

"No, thanks, Dad." Her voice was a whisper.

"What about you, Rell?"

I leaned back on the chair. "An egg burrito and an OJ would be great," I said.

"Can do," he said and threw LB a kiss.

"How you doing, Roomie?" I asked.

"I've been better." She smiled.

"You want some water?" There was a blue plastic pitcher on her nightstand.

"No thanks."

She saw me watch her click the morphine dispenser.

"It's for my chest," she said. "They put in a drainage tube

yesterday. It's a little hard to breathe."

I noticed bloodstains on her pillow and suspected they were from nosebleeds.

"Rell! I heard you were coming!" It was Mrs. Norman's voice. Mrs. Norman was one of the day nurses. "How are you doing, girl?" She clenched me to her king-sized-pillow chest.

I stiffened, pulling my neck back in a stretch to keep my wig from getting caught in her arms.

"Let me see you." She stood back and twirled her hand in the air.

One more spin of the body.

"You filled out quite nicely, young lady," she said. Mrs. Norman always smelled like baby powder. "I heard you've got yourself a boyfriend."

"Yes, Ma'm." Two minutes with Mrs. Norman and I fell into her North Carolina accent. "How did you know about my boyfriend?" I turned to LB and squinted my eyes.

"It was big news, Rell. I had to tell her," LB said.

Mrs. Norman scooted by me. She pushed the chair back with her shins. "I heard your beau is cute and smart." She adjusted LB's IV and checked the couplings on her chest tube.

"He's not really my boyfriend."

"Rell." It was Dr. Braden. He was in his green surgical scrubs, a sunflower cap and paper shoe booties. "How's my favorite Hawai'i patient?" Except for his gray hair, Dr. Braden looked like a football player. He had broad shoulders, big bones, a square jaw and intensely blue eyes the color of a cat's-eye marble.

"I'm your only Hawai'i patient." I beamed.

"It doesn't matter." He opened his arms and I hugged him, resting my cheek on his chest.

"You look well."

"Thanks."

"How's your mother?" He followed behind Mrs. Norman, checking LB's tube.

"She made you cream cheese brownies, but I forgot them in my room," I said.

"Don't tell him that," Mrs. Norman said. "He'll just send you over to get them."

"How's school?" He worked as he talked, making notes in LB's chart.

"A little rough at first, but it's getting easier."

"I heard you have a boyfriend. A nice young man."

I looked over at LB. She mouthed, "Sorry," to me.

"We're more like friends," I said.

"Does he get good grades?"

"Very good."

"And how about your grades?"

Mrs. Norman said, "You're beginning to sound more like her father than her doctor. Just leave the girl alone. You know she's got good sense."

He turned to her and said, "And you're beginning to sound like my wife." Dr. Braden took his stethoscope out of his pocket and swung it around his neck. "Rell, do you mind giving me a little time alone with LB?"

"Sure," I said. I knew the routine. "I'll be right down the hall." I waved to LB and stepped outside. I leaned my head against the tile walls, shut my eyes and let all the air out of my lungs. I felt like I just crossed the finish line of a ten-mile race.

"Rell!" I heard Mrs. Spencer, Jason's mom. "Rell, no one told me you were coming." She gave me a hug. "You look wonderful."

"Thanks."

"Are you back for follow-up tests?"

"No, to see LB."

"She's having a tough time of it," she said.

I nodded.

"Rell, it's so good to see you." She put her arm around my shoulder. "You've got to come down to see Jason." Mrs. Spencer steered me towards Jason's room.

"How's he doing?" I asked.

"Good. Dr. Lynch said he's responding well. Two more treatments and he should be ready to go home." She swung open the door to Jason's room. "Jas, look who's here."

Jason was sitting up in his bed watching his *All About Airplanes* video probably for the two hundredth time.

"Smelly Relly!"

"It's been a long time since anyone called me that," I said. I lumbered over to his bed. I hunched over, made my hands into claws and bared my teeth. "I'm going to get you," I groaned. "Ja-son!" I crept closer.

"No!" he screamed and billowed his sheets and scrambled underneath them.

"Ja-son!" I snarled my lips.

He didn't move.

"Ja-son!"

He peeked out from under his sheets. He took aim with

his finger and "shot" me. "I zapped you with my monster power," he said.

I clutched my chest, stood on my tiptoes, pivoted and fell to the floor. "You got me."

Jason beat his chest like a gorilla. His catheter protruded from his pajama tops. When I got up he said, "Rell, you still don't know how to die very well."

I stood up and put my hands on my hips. "Says who?"

"Says me." He pushed back his sheets and said, "This is how you play dead." He rolled on his back, bicycled his legs in the air, then flopped on his mattress like a griddle-cooked bacon.

"Next time, I'll do better." I said. I leaned over to kiss him.

"Rell, you got hair." He pointed to my Hat-Hair.

I lifted my wig to show him my real sprigs underneath. "Almost."

"Let me see." Mrs. Spencer came in for a closer look. "You are a regular long-haired beauty." She handed me a Play-Toy mirror.

The Rell I saw had thick eyebrows, pink skin and deep brown eyes flecked with gold.

"Rell, there's an eight year old diagnosed with Hodgkin's. She's here for treatment this week. Maybe you could introduce yourself."

"You want me to show her the 'After' photo?"

"Her name is Allyson. She's in 7-18."

That's when it hit me. I was one of the "returning patients" who I remembered when I was in treatment. They were the kids who visited the doctors and nurses and brought in boxes of candy and the photos of their proms—

the kids who were "cured"—the ones who were normal again.

Mr. O'Donnell peaked his head in Jason's room. He held up a cafeteria bag. "One egg burrito with OJ," he said.

"Thanks," I said and turned to Jason. "See you later, Jas." I headed back to LB's room. On the way, Dr. Braden stopped Mr. O'Donnell. He said he had the results of LB's tests. The two of them headed to Dr. Braden's office and I went in to see LB alone.

LB was sitting up, sipping water out of bottle. "You look great, Rell," she said.

"Thanks."

"Terrific makeup."

"My friend Emi taught me how to do it. I wrote you about it."

"It sounded like so much fun."

"It was no big deal." I didn't want to tell her about it and make her feel bad that I was doing normal things.

"What about that boyfriend of yours?" She took a sip of water.

I couldn't begin to tell her about Nate. "Things have changed."

"Good changed or bad changed?"

"Just different."

She clicked her morphine dispenser again.

"Do you have a limit on that stuff?" I asked.

"It's set high, so I always get a hit."

I settled in my chair and unwrapped my egg burrito. "Want some?" I offered LB.

She shook her head. "I don't eat much."

I asked her about the kids on the floor and she told me about the new crop of interns—which ones were cute and which ones thought they were real doctors.

"The cutest is Dr. Wallace." He was a redhead with braces.

"Rell, there's a small box in the top drawer of my dresser. Could you get it, please?"

It was from the Mule Shop in the Grand Canyon.

"Open it," she said.

It was LB's fire agate stone.

"My mom had it turned into a necklace for you."

The stone had flecks of gold and ripples of purple that smoked into gray.

"It would have been a great trip," she said.

We were both past pretending that it was going to happen.

"Read the brochure," she said.

I wiped my tears and unfolded the brochure. "The fire agate is a stone known for its healing properties. Shamans have used the fire agate during meditation because of its calming effects on the spirit. It is recommended to be worn as a talisman for healing."

"Sometimes the magic works and sometimes it doesn't." She shrugged.

I was afraid to hold her, she looked so frail. I put my arms around her shoulders, hoping I wasn't hurting her.

"I'm scared, Rell." She cried.

I pressed my cheek to hers. There were her tears and mine. And we held on to each other tight. I didn't want to let go of her. I knew it would be the last time I would hold her and if I let go it would be forever.

"Don't give up on miracles," I said.

"It's the only thing I have left."

I squatted down with my back to LB so she could put it on me. She had to reach over her tube to put it over my head.

"I'll never take it off," I said. "Never."

I turned around so she could see what it looked like on me.

"You're the one, Rell. You're going to beat the dragon."

Mr. O'Donnell opened the door. "Hey, Baby, I brought you a chocolate peppermint shake." He looked like he had been crying.

"Thanks Dad, but I'm not hungry."

"This isn't for hungry, it's for fun," Mr. O'Donnell said. "Take three sips and it's guaranteed to tickle your tummy like a tail thumpin' bunny."

"Oh, that was bad, Dad." LB groaned.

"Is Dr. Braden still outside?" I asked.

"He's at the nurses' station," he answered.

"I want to catch Dr. Braden before he leaves," I said to LB.

LB turned to her Dad, "See what your bad jokes do to people?"

Mr. O'Donnell and I switched places he could sit next to LB. "Don't worry, Rell, I have a lot worse jokes for when you get back."

Dr. Braden was walking down the hall when I caught up to him. "Do you have a minute?" I asked.

"Sure, what's up?"

"Can we go somewhere to talk?"

"My office?" he suggested.

"You bet."

I sat in the swivel chair next to his desk.

"What can I do for you, Rell?" he asked.

"Any word on the numbers?" When I was in treatment I would ask him that question when I wanted to know the survival rates were for kids who were getting my treatment. Right after I was diagnosed Mom, Dr. Braden and I discussed my treatment choices. We chose an experimental protocol from the University of South Florida.

"I read a report about two weeks ago," he said. "Stage IIA event-free survival rates were about 92 percent after five years."

Event free meant that no other cancers popped up, not even the kind that developed as a result of the treatment itself.

"It was a good choice," he said.

"Maybe not good enough."

"What do you mean?"

"I have a node."

His face turned serious. "Where?"

"In my neck." I reached up to touch it. "It's small but it's hard and it doesn't move."

"Have you seen Dr. Brice?"

Dr. Brice was the pediatric oncologist at Honolulu General.

"No, I wanted you to look at it first."

"And that was okay with your parents?"

"They don't know."

Dr. Braden swiveled his chair toward me. He rested his hands on his knees. "How long have you had it?"

"A few days. Maybe a week."

"Rell, you should have told your parents right away."

"I didn't want to worry them. I figured you could take a look and if it's nothing they'd never have to know."

"Rell, this is your life we're talking about."

"I know," I said. "But I knew I was going to see you."

"Rell, I can't treat you. Not without your parents' permission."

"I don't want you to treat me," I said. "I just want you to feel my neck."

"I can't. Not without their permission."

"It doesn't have to be anything official."

He reached for the phone. "What's your number? I can give your mom a call and that would do it for now."

I pushed his hand down. "Don't!" Instantly I realized what I had done. "Don't," I said it again; this time it was more like a pleading. "My mother worries." My voice cracked. "I don't want her to know yet—not if it's nothing."

"Rell, have you had any night sweats?"

"No."

"Fever? Weight loss? Rashes?"

"No. Nothing except the node."

Dr. Braden's pager went off. "Rell, I'm going to have to call your parents."

"Why?"

"I have to inform them." He checked his pager.

I thought I could trust you.

"I'll tell them. I promise." I wasn't sure if I really would.

"When are you leaving for Hawai`i?"

"The day after tomorrow," I said.

"Rell, if you've relapsed, the quicker you get back into

treatment the better." He tapped his desk as he spoke.

"Do you think my cancer is back?"

"I don't know."

"And you won't check me?"

"If I had permission I would do it right now." His pager went off again.

All I wanted him to do was to feel my neck, because I knew that he could tell if the cancer was back just by feeling it.

"This isn't a game, Rell." He checked his pager again. Then he looked at his calendar. "I'll give you until Friday. On Friday I'll be calling your house to find out what's going on."

When I went back to LB's room, Mrs. O'Donnell was standing in the hallway.

"Rell." She took me in her arms. "Thank you for coming." It was the first time I had seen her since I was at Stanhope. The fluorescent light made her skin look pale and it reflected a silver halo at the base of her black-dyed hair.

"You okay?" She, too, looked like she had been crying.

"Dr. Braden just gave us some bad news. The cancer spread to her spine. It's in the base of her skull."

"It's in her spine." I repeated her words and I bobbed my head like a ceramic doll on the dashboard of a car. "Does she know?"

"I just told her."

Another rigid order from my brain: Do not show any emotion.

"Rell, I can't believe this is happening." Mrs. O'Donnell twisted a tissue between her fingers. "I kept saying to myself that she was going to beat this thing. I really believed it. But…." She shrugged and started to cry. I put my arms around her and she sobbed, burying her head in my chest. It was strange to have an adult cry in my arms.

"Hang tough," I heard her say. Then she pulled herself back and pushed her hair back. She took a deep breath and said, "Rell, could you sit with LB for awhile? Mr. O'Donnell and I need to talk."

When I went in her room, LB's eyes were closed. Whether she was asleep or just closing herself off to the world didn't matter. I just sat, watching her breathe—fast, shallow gasps, almost panting. My eyes were glued to her chest. I thought if I just keep watching her, her breathing won't stop.

She opened her eyes and looked over at me, "I'm not going to make it, Rell."

Where were the Angels of Mercy that guarded the beds of children?

"Are you afraid?" I whispered.

"I'm not afraid of being dead. I'm afraid of dying."

I could feel tears flowing down my cheeks.

"Miracles happen, LB. You can't give up hope."

"I'm going to die hoping, Rell." Then she closed her eyes and drifted back to sleep.

I sat in the chair next to her bed. I curled my legs up and wrapped myself up as tight as I could, twisitng the hospital blanket around me like a shield. I looked over at

LB. It was like her body had already let go and only her spirit was hanging on.

Where are you, God?

I knew I wouldn't get an answer.

Once at Stanhope, LB told me she thought we were the lucky ones—all of us in treatment—because we were being treated for cancer, while the other kids, the normal kids, didn't know they had it and were walking around with it eating their insides away.

I hated cancer and I hated a God that let it happen. Mrs. Norman used to say that God takes back the special angels to be close to him. *What kind of selfish God would do that?* Whenever I saw pictures of God surrounded by young children, I never pictured the kids as being dead.

LB was going to die and there wasn't a thing I could do about it. I wished I had special words to say to her—some poem with words so beautiful that they should be written in gold calligraphy. But I had no words and I was running out of prayers.

When LB's parents came back in her room, they adjusted her bed, plumped up her pillows, filled her pitcher with water, rearranged the magazines on her tray, smoothed her sheets. Mr. O'Donnell paced back and forth with his hands in his pockets, rattling the loose change. Mrs. O'Donnell folded towels. And LB slept, unaware.

As I watched Mrs. O'Donnell I remembered my mother folding towels and smoothing my sheets, adjusting the shades to keep the sun out of my eyes. And as I watched, I began to understand what it must have been like for her.

I walked down the hall. I wanted to go home. I never wanted to see a doctor or a nurse again. I strolled through the lobby, browsed the gift shop, sat in the chapel and walked the parking lot before I ended up in the cafeteria.

Hospital cafeterias have a sameness to them—staff in scrubs discussing patients while they eat, doctors jumping up when their names are paged, patients in wheelchairs with IVs swinging from poles, families huddled at tables. I got in line and slid my tray across the stainless steel tube shelf, past counters of deep-fried foods and heated kiosks of pizza. I ordered a salad. It had brown-tinged lettuce leaves and hard yellow-orange tomatoes. I poured myself a Diet Coke.

I picked up a *San Francisco Happenings* newspaper and sat at a far table next to the window. The cafeteria added a coffee cart since I had left. It was decorated like a cable car and had a brass coffee urn. There was a patient in line that looked like Tess. She was in a wheelchair and was wearing a tie-dyed turban on her head. After Tess died I was sure I saw her alive. Once I thought she was a girl at the outpatient radiology clinic, but when the girl turned around, it wasn't Tess. Another time I thought I saw her at the Laundromat at the Hospitality House. After a while it stopped happening.

I headed back to LB's room. She was asleep, and I was glad. It was easier for me. I walked the grounds of the hospital until dusk then headed back to the Hospitality House. I had no sense of time. I know I microwaved a dinner at the house kitchen then I went back to my room and turned on the TV, but I can't remember what I watched. I wasn't thinking. I wasn't feeling much either. I was numb. Then I fell asleep.

I dreamed about LB. The two of us were dancing—swirling through banners of yellow and green. A banjo played, a fiddler kept time. We were locked arm-in-arm.

Someone called, "Faster the flute. Faster the banjo. Faster the fiddler's thumb." A young girl sang, "Throw over the veil. Throw open the sky. Your friend has gone to God."

I woke up panting. My heart pounded. It was three o'clock in the morning and I was afraid to call LB's room and afraid to go back to sleep. I put on the TV and sat up in bed, but somehow I fell asleep until morning.

The reality of morning was worse than any dream. I was standing in LB's room when she had a seizure. I watched her body shake. Her mother ran for a nurse. Her father held her shoulders down.

"Hold on," I whispered, holding the fire agate tight in my hand.

Her body convulsed. Once more. Then another spasm. Then quiet. My knees quivered. Two nurses ran in. Please, no. I didn't want to see what they would do to her. I ran outside, pressed my back against the tile wall and let myself go, sliding down the wall until I was crouched on the floor with my knees to my chest.

A doctor flew into LB's room, another nurse followed, and then Mrs. Norman ran in. I put my head down. I didn't want to know. I could hear them calling out orders. Slowly, I got up and looked in the window.

LB's mom covered her face with her hands. She was rocking. Mr. O'Donnell was holding her up.

Please, God, make it all go away.

Mrs. Norman came out and put her arms around me.

"How's LB? I asked her.

"She's a tough little angel. She made it through." Mrs. Norman said they were "to be expected" and would become more frequent. She never said "then she'll die," but I knew that's what would happen. I didn't want LB to die, not like that, with her body shaking and everybody rushing around her. If she had to die, I wanted it to be peaceful.

When I went back in her room, she was resting, half-asleep. She opened her eyes and said, "Rell, one minute I fight as hard as I can and the next I want to give up trying." She clicked the morphine dispenser and closed her eyes.

Her body rattled a few more times but she never woke up. It was like there was a battle going on—like her body and her soul were fighting and neither one was giving up.

I stretched out my arms and unfolded my legs and got up to walk around. My legs were asleep. I patted the pins-and-needles feeling away and walked in circles in front of LB's nightstand. I noticed a Book of Prayers laying on it. Next to it was an index card with something written in LB's handwriting. It was a poem by Carl Sandburg.

Loosen your hands,

Let go and say goodbye.

Let the stars and the songs go.

Loosen your hands and say goodbye.

I didn't want to let go of the stars. I wanted to rip them

from the sky with the moon and tie them with a silver bow, making them into a bouquet that could give LB back her life.

On my last day at Stanhope LB's energy soared. She was sitting up, laughing, telling jokes. It terrified me because right before Tess died, she rallied, too.

Mr. O'Donnell ordered a deep-dish pizza from Aunty Lina's in North Beach.

"Do I smell pizza?" Jason's mom wheeled him in.

"Pizza!" Jason squealed. "Pizz-ah! Beast-ah! Feast-ah!" Jason had discovered rhyme. His mom tied a blue plastic bib over his pajamas—chemo ports had to be kept clean.

LB pointed to the pizza boxes on her dresser. "Dad got an extra mushroom and sausage for you. The one with anchovies is for Mrs. Norman."

We passed around packets of cheese and wiped streaks of tomato sauce off our cheeks. I took a bite of my pizza, stretching the cheese out toward the ceiling. "Aunty Lina's makes the best pizza. Too bad they don't deliver to Hawai'i."

"Can you see it?" LB said. "One thousand 'plane pizzas' to go." She extended her arms like airplane wings and tilted them to the right. "Get it? Plane pizzas?"

Her mother moaned. Her father beamed, "That's my girl."

"Proof that bad joke telling is hereditary," her mom said.

They were teasing each other like they were a regular family and the delivery boy just dropped off a pizza to their house like it was a regular Wednesday afternoon.

I checked my watch. It was getting closer to the time I had to leave. LB checked the wall clock. About ten minutes before I had to go, LB's mom cleared everyone out of the room but me.

I held LB's hand.

"Promise me you'll get to the Grand Canyon, Rell."

"Absolutely."

"And hike all the way to the bottom."

"Can't I take a tour bus?" I said.

"You hike. All the way down and you think of me every step of the way."

"I can think of you in an air-conditioned bus," I said. I looked up at the ceiling to keep my tears from falling.

"No," she said. "And promise me that you're going to tell me all about it. And you're going to tell me about school and Nate, and when you get married and have babies I want to know every little detail. Even if you think I can't hear you, I'll be listening." She started to cry and cupped her palms over her eyes gently. "Do you remember what it felt like to cry without eyelashes?" She was both laughing and crying.

I grinned and nodded.

"You know the worst part of it, Rell? I'll never know what was supposed to happen to me. I wish I could fast forward my life to find out, and then rewind it back to now. I just want to know."

"I love you, LB," I said.

"Right back at you, Roomie."

Those were the last words she said to me.

CHAPTER TEN

Before leaving for the airport I stopped by to see Dr. Braden. There was a young doctor waiting in his office. He had red hair and braces.

It must be the new intern.

"Hi," I said.

"Hi. I'm Dr. Wallace."

"Is Dr. Braden around?" I asked.

"He should be here soon. We're supposed to discuss one of my patients."

One of his patients. He was definitely an intern.

"I was a patient of Dr. Braden," I said. "Hodgkin's, Stage IIA." They always wanted to know your diagnosis. "I came back a couple of days ago."

He furled his eyebrows. "When did you relapse?"

I almost said, "I didn't," but I figured if he thought I had relapsed I could get him to check my neck. "A couple of weeks ago. I have a node in my neck." I angled my ear to my shoulder. "Would you like to feel it?" Interns loved to make their own diagnoses.

He stood in front of me and pulsed his fingers over my neck. He had a gentle touch, not like most interns. He firmly pressed back and forth around the node. Then he felt under my jaw line and down toward my collarbone.

"Do you feel it?" I asked.

"Here." He put his finger right over it.

"That's it," I said.

"It does feel suspicious."

"Dr. Wallace!" Dr. Braden walked in.

Dr. Wallace startled. He seemed as afraid as I was.

"Wait for me in the conference room," Dr. Braden said.

I knew what I did was bad, beyond bad, maybe it was even illegal. But I didn't care. I had to know.

"Don't get mad at him. It was my fault," I said.

"I'll talk to him later."

"I tricked him," I said.

"Just exactly what did you expect to happen?" Dr. Braden sat in his chair, legs spread, resting his elbows on his knees.

"I wanted somebody to check my node," I said. "And now I know it's back."

"From a diagnosis from an intern!" He reached into his lab coat and pulled out a pen. "What's your home phone number?" He copied it down then called. I sat there as he explained to Mom what I had just done. The last thing he said to her was, "I'll take a look at her now."

"Come on, Rell. You're going to get your wish." He escorted me into an examination room.

I lied down on the examining table and closed my eyes. I didn't want to look at his face. I knew I was wrong but I needed to know. If he had just felt my neck to begin with, none of this would have happened.

"Right here?" His fingers were directly over it.

"Yes."

He said, "Swallow." I swallowed. "Again." I swallowed again. "Turn to the left," he said, and I did.

He did it all again, then he went to the sink and washed

his hands.

"Is it back?" I asked.

"I can't say without further tests."

It's back.

"Is it suspicious?" I asked.

"Dr. Brice will be doing some tests."

My flight home arrived in Honolulu at three o'clock. By four-thirty Dad was pulling into Honolulu General Hospital's parking lot. There was an uneasy feeling on the ride over. Mom and Dad were forged together. It was like they joined forces to wage war against cancer. It was like the silence in our house when I was first diagnosed. The same but different. This time we all knew what we were facing.

The three of us got in the elevator. "Two, please," Mom said.

The doors opened into the Pediatric Oncology reception area. The three of us sat in a line, on blue tweed chairs that were bolted to the floor. CNN was on the TV. The TV was bolted to the ceiling. Next to it was a photo collage of "Cancer Hall of Fame." I remembered the first time I saw it. It was when my family doctor sent me to see Dr. Brice because he suspected that I had cancer. I remembered looking at the photos thinking I didn't belong on that board. That was a board for kids who were going to die. My photo still wasn't up there. It was at Stanhope on a bulletin board next to the nurses' station.

Dr. Brice welcomed us into his office. He was about seventy, with steel gray eyes and a tight gray crew cut. He wore a white lab coat, a blue shirt and a maroon-and-gold striped tie. "This is

Dr. Alaire. She's a pediatric oncology resident." Dr. Alaire had wavy auburn hair pulled back in a French braid. She had deep green eyes and a warm smile.

Dr. Brice began in a matter-of-fact voice. "Dr. Braden and I have consulted extensively. He faxed me Rell's complete record, and we have talked at length." He flipped through papers on his desk. "Her last test results look good. Her blood work has been excellent."

I held on to LB's agate while Dr. Brice shifted more papers.

"Dr. Braden and I are in agreement that an FNA is the best course."

Mom nodded. Dad asked what an FNA was.

"Fine needle aspiration. It's a simple procedure." Dr. Brice folded his hands as he spoke. His hands were gnarled and covered with age spots, and I wondered how sensitive they were. "The surgeon inserts a needle into the tumor and extracts some cells, which are examined for any abnormalities. It's done with a topical anesthetic. It's quite painless."

"When will you do it?" Dad asked.

"We have it scheduled for tomorrow morning at seven."

Dad crossed his legs. He tapped his thighs with his thumb. "When do we get the results?"

"The next day," Dr. Brice said.

Dad jiggled his foot. "Do you think this is cancer?" Dad taking the direct approach.

"Mr. DeMello, girls Rell's age commonly have swollen lymph nodes. Most of them never even notice them. And, if it were not for Rell's medical history, this node would be of no concern to me."

"So it's probably not cancer." Dad needing guarantees.

"We don't know," Dr. Brice said.

"I thought Hodgkin's disease was a curable cancer." He needed control.

"Mr. DeMello, we have been quite successful treating Hodgkin's disease." Dr. Brice was making no commitment.

"You know Rell was treated at Stanhope." Dad leaned forward. "It's the best hospital in the country for Hodgkin's."

He knows that, Dad.

"Mr. DeMello, despite our best efforts, sometimes patients relapse."

He said it.

Dad slumped. Mom reached for his hand.

Then Dr. Alaire spoke, "Mr. DeMello, the prognosis for Hodgkin's patients is excellent. Even if Rell has relapsed, her prognosis would still be quite good."

I smiled at her. She smiled back.

"For all we know, this could be a reactive node. Nothing to worry about," she said.

Dad was unsmiling.

"So, Rell, why don't we get started?" Dr. Alaire led me into an examining room and readied me for Dr. Brice. Dr. Alaire was first to examine me while Dr. Brice supervised her. Then he checked me. His touch was light and gentle. I watched them as they worked, alert for any clue as to what they thought—a pitying glance, a momentary stare between them — any sign to tell me if they thought my cancer was back.

"Okay, Rell," Dr. Alaire said. "We're finished for the day."

"We will see you bright and early tomorrow," Dr. Brice

said. I thought I heard a rehearsed casualness in his voice. It made me afraid.

On the way home Dad weaved through traffic. He tailgated, sped and drove through the stop sign at the end of our street, then he cut a steep angle into our driveway.

As we walked to the front door he put his arm around me. "Whatever happens, we're going to get through this," he said. "All of us. One step at a time."

We were going to face cancer as a family.

That day was the longest day of my life. It started in San Francisco, at Stanhope. I woke up, had pizza with LB and told her goodbye. That morning Dr. Braden still trusted me, my parents didn't know anything about my node and I wasn't scheduled for any procedures. By nightfall, my life was spinning out of control. There was nothing to hold on to. Nothing had stayed the same.

After dinner I called Nate. Our fighting was becoming routine.

"I can't believe you pulled a stunt like that. What the hell were you thinking talking to an intern? You know more about cancer than any intern."

"I needed to know," I said.

"What did Dr. Braden do?"

"He called my mother. I didn't think he would."

"What did you expect him to do?" I could picture him shaking his head, disgusted by my illogic. "What happens next?" Nate asked.

"I'm scheduled for an FNA at Honolulu General."

"Why an FNA? Why don't they cut the whole thing out?"

"It's not necessary."

"You need a second opinion, Rell. Get an aggressive doc on your side. You're caving in."

"Dr. Braden talked to Dr. Brice. They both think the same thing."

"Get another opinion."

So I can hear it all again?

"I don't want another opinion."

"You've got to take control of your life, Rell."

"Stop it, Nate."

"This is typical of you. You live in a fairy-tale world, Rell. You think you can have an FNA and everything will go away."

"It isn't your call."

"You know they can miss it. One part of the node can be cancerous, and they can miss it."

"I know."

"Why don't you do something about it?"

I was totally beaten down.

"I've got to go, Nate."

"Rell, you can't roll over on this."

"I can't deal with this right now."

"Rell, this is important."

"Good-bye, Nate."

I hung up.

The next morning Mom came in my room twice to get me up. I did everything I could to make us late. I took a slow shower and I got dressed even slower, but they still got me to the hospital on time. At seven a.m. I was lying on an examining table in the treatment room at Honolulu

General.

The surgeon introduced himself. "Good morning, Rell. I'm Dr. Williams."

I was lying on a padded table. I had on jeans and a green-paper hospital top.

"This is something to relax you," Dr. Williams said. It was an injection, not an IV.

A second surgeon came in. She, too, had on a mask, cap and gloves. She introduced herself as Dr. Carol. The first thing she did was to ask Mom and Dad to leave the room. Dad asked her to keep the door open and they did.

Dr. Williams rolled a tray of instruments to within their reach. He pulled down the square fluorescent light. "You're going to have to take your necklace off," he said.

"Can't I just move it out of the way?" I asked.

"Sorry," was the answer.

I took it off and clutched it in my hand.

The doctors leaned over me. Dr. Williams pulled the light even closer. I shut my eyes as he probed my neck.

"How are you feeling?" he asked.

"Woozy," I said.

"Good. It'll be over soon."

I heard him say, "Here, Carol, near the tattoo." When I was in treatment my neck was tattooed with small dots marking the corner of where I got my radiation.

"Okay, Rell, you should feel quite relaxed now," Dr. Carol said.

The music played. Faster the fiddle. Faster the drum.

"You got it, Carol?"

Faster the banjo.

"You're going to feel a little pressure, Rell," she said.

Let go the flute. Let go the drum.

"Almost done," he said.

"Almost done," she said.

"Yes, almost," he echoed.

I felt a tug. It was like a rubber band stretching inside my neck, then a sting and some pressure, then I heard them both exhale.

"It's over, Rell."

For them.

I was dazed and still woozy. When I got home I slept until noon, when I got up and Dad made pancakes for lunch. I watched TV, talked to Emi. But all I really was doing was waiting.

It would be twenty-four hours before Dr. Brice would have the test results. I hated the waiting. Waiting was when you imagined the worst.

What's stronger, fear or hope?

Nate never called.

About eight o'clock I heard the phone ring. Mom answered. I could hear part of her conversation. She walked down the hall into my room and sat on my bed. "Mrs. O'Donnell called." I knew the next thing she was going to say. "LB died this afternoon."

I said, "Okay." I couldn't absorb anymore.

I drifted down through my bed, through the floor, down into the ground, past the fire, into a void where there was absolutely nothing left.

"Do you want me to sit with you awhile?" Mom asked.

"No, I'm okay," I said and rolled over, trying not to feel.

But the rage seeped out, rolled out, surged and crashed and dug deep inside me.

Let go the stars. Throw over the veil.

I gripped the agate hard. LB is dead. What followed in my head was "And you could be next."

I heard the doctors' words: "Normal, reactive node. Suspicious." I punched in my pillow. Sobs with no sound. I wanted to rip the node right out of my neck, just dig it out with my nails.

This isn't fair! I had a deal. I beat cancer. I already beat it once. I can't have it twice. It's not fair.

There was no one left who could understand. Tess was gone, now so was LB.

I grabbed the phone and called Nate. There was no answer. I tried his cell phone. Nothing. I dialed again. Nothing.

I called Emi. "Where's Nate?"

"At Paul's brother's frat house. Why?"

"Emi, you've got to take me there." I was desperate.

"Wait. What happened in San Francisco?"

"LB died," I said.

"I'm sorry, Rell. Do you want me to come over?"

"No. I need to see Nate."

"Can't you talk to me?"

"Not for this."

"Rell, I don't think this is a good idea."

"I have to see him." I started to cry.

"Okay. I'll be right there."

Emi was at my house in minutes, and soon she was turning the corner on the frat house street. The road was lined with cars. Some kids were sitting on the front lawn drinking. Music was blasting from the house.

"Are you sure you don't want me to go in with you?"
Emi asked.

"I'll be okay."

"What if you need a ride home?"

"I'll call you." I ran to the house.

"Rell," she yelled from the car.

"I'm okay."

The living room was crowded and heavy with smoke.
There were couples everywhere dancing, standing, lying in
chairs with their legs intertwined. I spotted Nate on the
other side of the room and forged a path to him past
dancing couples grinding their hips together.

"What are you doing here?" he asked.

"I need to talk to you."

"Hi." A guy next to Nate, about six foot three with a
shaved head, lifted his beer bottle toward me.

"Did you get your test results?" Nate asked.

"No."

"I need to talk to you."

"Go home, Rell."

"I came to talk."

"Look around." He waved his beer bottle in the air. "This
isn't a place to talk. How did you even know I was here?"

"Emi."

The guy next to Nate with the shaved head was staring
at me. He had a copper goatee and green eyes.

"You're the only one who understand. I need you," I said.

"Everything is a crisis with you, Rell."

"Why are you being so mean?"

"Because I'm an asshole, remember?"

"I'm scared," I pleaded.

"Not scared enough." He jabbed his beer in the air. "What good is an FNA? Two months from now you could be facing the same thing and then they'll do a biopsy. Rell, you've got to have the guts to face this thing." He shook his head. "You're just playing games."

"I thought you would understand. But you just keep everything in your damn little boxes."

"I face things, Rell."

"No, you put them away."

The guy with the shaved head watched the whole thing.

"You need to talk. Then talk," Nate said.

I wanted to scream at him that LB was dead. Yell it out for everyone to hear. But I said, "Never mind."

"Gladly." Nate started to walk away.

The guy with the shaved head walked up to me. "You look like you could use a beer."

"Thanks." I took it.

"I'm Blaine. Nate and I play basketball together, but he's never mentioned his girlfriend."

"I'm not his girlfriend," I said. "And my name is Rell."

"Like the surfer?"

"In more ways than one."

Rell Sunn, one of Hawai'i's greatest surfers, died of breast cancer.

"Do you surf?" Blaine leaned his arm over the wall behind me, towering over my five-foot-four body.

Nate backtracked. "Since when did you start drinking?"

"Since now," I answered.

"Go home, Rell," Nate said.

I looked directly at Blaine. "No, I don't surf. I never even tried."

"You certainly have the body for it." Up close his goatee reflected a copper stubble.

I took a sip of my beer as Nate watched.

Nate pulled the beer from my hand. "She's fifteen, Blaine. She shouldn't be drinking."

"Relax, Nate. One beer's not going to kill a fifteen year old."

"That's right," I said. "It isn't beer that kills fifteen year olds."

"All I'm offering here is a surfing lesson and a midnight swim." Blaine took a slight bow. "A perfectly gentlemanly proposition."

Nate put his arm around me like he was staking a claim. "Stay out of this, Blaine."

"Sorry, Nate, she said you weren't together."

I lifted Nate's arm off me. "We're not!"

Blaine held his hands up in surrender. "Hey, I don't want to get in the middle of a domestic argument," he said.

"I *said* I'm not with him. He thinks I play things too safe. Isn't that right, Nate? I'm too afraid to face things." I turned to Blaine. "Is that offer for surfing still good?"

He nodded.

"Then let's go."

Blaine looked at Nate.

"Go," he said. "You deserve whatever you get."

Blaine snatched a six-pack off the table and tucked it under his arm. He took my hand and we ran down the street to his Camaro. I hopped in the front seat.

Blaine popped open two cans of beer. We tapped our cans together and chugged them down. Blaine pounded the steering wheel with his fist. "Let's surf!"

He sped down the quarry road, taking the curves tightly. I leaned into him. The radio blasted. I sang along with the music. I echoed Blaine's "Par-tee!" screaming and drinking like I did it all the time.

"Have you ever shot the tunnel?" he asked.

I shook my head.

"A tunnel virgin!"

Blaine swerved up the Pali Road doing sixty, maybe seventy miles an hour. He reeled from one lane to another. Then right before the tunnel, he jerked the steering wheel. We were driving into the oncoming tunnel!

He blasted the horn. The blare ricocheted off the walls. I couldn't scream. I braced my hands against the dashboard. My elbows locked. My legs tensed.

Oncoming car!

He hit the brakes. We fishtailed. He yanked the steering wheel, jumped on the accelerator. We were skidding — sideways. We were facing the tunnel wall. Spinning. Skidding. The brakes squealed. Another spin. We veered right. Brakes.

We were out of the tunnel. Blaine cut across two lanes. Gravel. Brakes. Then we stopped in a cloud of gray smoke.

My hands were still clamped on the dashboard. My elbows still locked.

Blaine threw his fists high over his head, laughing. "Yes!"

"You almost killed us."

Blaine leaned over and stroked my cheek with his finger,

"Babe, I gave you the ride of your life."

"Don't."

Blaine drew me closer. "Come on, Rell. You loved it."

I reached behind myself for the door.

He gripped the back of my neck. "I was just having a little fun." He stroked my cheek with his tongue.

"Let go!"

"Relax, pretty girl." He kissed the back of my neck.

I tried to break loose. He pulled me in tighter. "I guess you really are a real tunnel virgin." He started to climb on top of me. "But Old Blaine's going to take care of that."

I got the door open and ran.

Blaine got out of the car. He leaned on the roof. "There's nowhere to go, Rell."

I scrambled up the hill. He started after me. I slipped on the gravel. He was catching up.

"Come on down, Rell. We're wasting good lovin' time."

I took in ragged breaths.

"Come on, Rell."

I kept running.

"Come out, come out, wherever you are." He was singing.

I hobbled to my feet.

"Hey, pretty baby, I'll make you feel so good."

"Leave me alone," I yelled. "I called Nate. He's on his way."

"You're lying."

"I'm not."

"He's coming."

"We'll be through before he gets here."

There was a ledge. I was trapped. There was no place to go.

"Shit!" I heard Blaine fall.

I saw him double over, holding his knee.

"911. I just called 911," I shouted. "The police will be here."

Blaine was staggering.

"They're coming."

"You want to stay out here?" he yelled. "Go ahead. You can die out here for all I care."

I watched as he dragged his leg down the hill. When Blaine was far enough away, I fumbled through my purse and called Nate. Then I waited, crouched down behind a clump of bamboo trees.

When Blaine got back in his car, I edged down the hill. I could hear the motor running. He was sitting there.

Where are you, Nate?

Cars roared out of the tunnel. I could feel their blasts. The exhaust gagged me. My stomach contracted in spasms. I was so afraid. I kneeled over and threw up then I wiped my face with my shirt and hid until I saw Nate's truck. He swerved into the emergency lot and as soon as he peeled in, Blaine tore out.

I ran to him.

He grabbed my shoulders. "Did he hurt you?"

"No." I was still shaking.

"Did anything happen?"

I shook my head.

"Rell, did he do *anything* to you?"

"No." I covered my face and buried myself into his arms.

"Are you okay?"

"No." He helped me in the car.

We drove back to Kailua, through the Pali tunnel. I saw my face reflected in the windshield in the tunnel's lights. My cheeks were streaked with mascara, my wig was muddied and my lipstick was smeared on my chin.

"You need to get cleaned up before you go home," he said. "Lanikai beach should be open."

Nate stopped at the fishermen's pier at Lanikai Beach. The restrooms were open.

Nate waited for me on the jetty.

After I got myself together, I sat next to him on the rocks. "I'm sorry."

Nate tossed pebbles into the crevices between the boulders.

"It's been a lousy few days," I said.

He didn't look up.

"LB died," I said. "It happened this afternoon."

"I'm sorry, Rell."

A black crab scampered down the crevice.

"It's okay," I said.

And we went back to tossing pebbles.

"Rell, do you remember when you asked me if I ever thought my cancer was back?"

I nodded.

"I never answered you." He stopped tossing the pebbles. "At the end of seventy weeks of treatment I had a full battery of tests. One of them came back with 'suspicious' results. It took me a week to get a clean bill of health— after seventy weeks of treatment, there was the chance that none of it mattered and I was going to die anyway."

"What did you do?"

"I got stupid and I got beat up a lot," he said. "I picked fights with the biggest guys I could find. I wanted to pummel somebody or something, but I really wanted to them to pummel me."

"Did it work?"

"I got beat up a lot." He smiled.

I reached for his hand.

"I picked on some very big guys. But, no, it didn't work."

"Did anything work?"

"My grandmother called me. She said, 'Nathan, life isn't fair. Life just is.'"

"That's not good enough for me," I said. "I want life to be perfect. Every day perfect—and I want guarantees."

I thought he was going to tell me "move on" or "get over it," but he didn't. He said, "Life's not perfect, Rell. And you got dealt a lousy hand. But what do you think LB would give to be in your shoes?"

The next morning in Dr. Brice's office Mom, Dad and I sat in straight-backed chairs waiting for my test results. Dr. Brice's report was brief. "There is no evidence of cancer."

I didn't want to break the spell. *"No evidence of cancer."*

"The node appears normal. We will watch it closely, but given all the other information we have, I am confident that Rell will be fine."

"So the node is not cancer?" Dad needed hard answers.

"Mr. DeMello, without completely removing the node and doing a biopsy, I can't guarantee that it isn't cancerous. What I can say is that a team of physicians reviewed Rell's case and we all believe this to be a normal reactive node."

Mom cried. Dad shook Dr. Brice's hand.

If my life were a movie, it would have ended right then. The credits would have rolled by and there would have been a shift to a scene at the beach. Violins would play, waves would lap and there would be a wide-angle shot of me running in the sand.

I would have my face to the sun, stretching my arms over my head. A silk scarf would billow in the breeze. The camera would pan out across the ocean, and at the end of the credits there would be a still frame and the following words would be on the screen: "Estrella DeMello was cured of cancer." And it would give a specific date.

But that's not how real life works. In real life I tried to forget I had cancer, but that never worked. It took a long time for me to figure out that having cacner was part of who I was. It's what happened to me when I was fifteen.

That was ten years ago. I'm twenty-five now and I'm sitting at Kailua beach. The sky is overcast and there's a slight rain, so I found an iron tree to sit under to keep dry as I sit watching a frigate bird soar by.

A few surfers are bobbing in the ocean, straddling their boards. They look like they're waiting for a perfect wave. I want to tell them that there are no perfect waves, just ordinary waves. Just like there are not perfect lives and there are no perfect days. There are only ordinary days—gloriously wonderful, shared and remembered, celebrated and cherished—miracles of ordinary days.